ALTAR OF FLESH
PRINCE OF LUST
BOOK III

LUCIEN BURR

ALTAR OF FLESH
Lucien Burr

Edited by Drew McBlain

Cover Art by 4RESNA

Book Design by Lucien Burr

Ebook design by Lucien Burr

This book is a work of fiction and as such all characters and situations are fictitious. Any resemblance to actual people, places or events is coincidental.

Category (Adult Erotic Fiction)
Genre (Paranormal/ Romance / LGBT)

CONTENT WARNINGS

Occult, submission and dominance, physical abuse, moral degradation, religious themes, religious mockery, extreme sexual activity, vomiting, bleeding, prolapse, borderline zoophilic monsters, CNC, use of knife/light self-harm

Please note:

All sigils are in the public domain.

Original source: THE BOOK OF THE GOETIA OF SOLOMON THE KING (1904), S.L. MacGregor Mathers and Aleister Crowley

PROLOGUE

"BUT EVERY MAN IS TEMPTED,
WHEN HE IS DRAWN AWAY
OF HIS OWN LUST, AND
ENTICED."

James 1:14

"HE THAT HATH NO RULE OVER
HIS OWN SPIRIT IS LIKE A
CITY THAT IS BROKEN
DOWN, AND WITHOUT
WALLS."

Proverbs 25:28

Vulnerable like a city without walls, waiting for a conquering.

If my holiness at any point could be akin to godliness, if my faith at any point might bestow sanctity upon my body, I was at that moment Jerusalem with its broken walls, open to evil. Perhaps what separated me from Nehemiah and his great distress over Jerusalem's defencelessness was the love I possessed for my weakness.

I was delectably susceptible. A willing, stupid man who had abandoned God so completely that I no longer heard even the slightest tug of his call. Lying in the ejaculate of demons, with my hole spent and leaking, I could think of nothing else except *holy, holy, holy*.

The way God led Nehemiah to rebuild Jerusalem's wall or Ezra to the temple, I felt like He had led me to this.

Fear not. I still possessed an ear for blasphemy. I knew at once that my feelings were human and ridiculous, that under no circumstance would God have allowed this—even as a means of returning me to His flock. Yet a kind of peace had taken root in me, orgasmic in its pervasiveness. It was as if every fuck encouraged another sprouting branch, another knotted root system that fed me euphoria, joy, desire, lust. I had no use for shame any longer.

Not after I had found my purpose.

❧ I ❧
CHAPTER ONE

The two untamed demons left me in a mess of our combined fluids. I do not recall how much time passed. Something as ephemeral as time and how it slipped by felt impossible to comprehend in a place like Hell; things happened, or they didn't, and I did not grow hungry or particularly tired. The exhaustion that did come was less physical than mental, and even that came in waves. But I found I could not sleep, as if my stamina revitalised itself over time without me needing to do anything.

In this sense, it became difficult to do much except think and, in thinking, fantasise. I recall after a bout of languid, far-away dreaming, where I dreamed in earnest about the demons that had violated me, I finally came back to myself and my body.

Around me, there was only desolation. The mirage of a church in which I had been so thoroughly destroyed had peeled away. The only evidence of what had happened to me was the fluids I laid in and the wounds in my hands and feet —though even these were already beginning to heal. Stickiness clung to my skin, and warmth pooled throughout my body and organs. Never before had such euphoria filled me. It was as if everything in me had come together: no longer was I a lost lamb but a man imbued with purpose.

My body ached in a pleasant way, and distantly, I recall feeling glad I could still feel things such as pain and discomfort, not only during sex but afterwards. Pleasure became all the more beautiful for it.

I looked down at the open wounds in my palms, the stigmata, and pressed my thumbs into the puckered wounds. Stinging pain hissed through my palm, and I pulled my finger away. I tried not to think about Christ. I tried not to compare myself to Him and his holiness, especially when my insides grew hot; this arousal towards pain was a new development.

It was my ego. My ego had poisoned my own well. Something about knowing I could never quite die had encouraged this perverse arousal. I could be pushed to my mortal limits, tested and encouraged along to my breaking point, and it made the promise of pain alluring.

Reborn as I was, having been baptised in milky unholiness, and with Asmodeus on my mind, I pushed myself up. I staggered away from the mess the three of us had made and walked for a long while. Once again, Hell became a nothingness, a desert of structure and direction. But I let my heart lead me, holding my purpose out like a beacon. To be Asmodeus' pet, its hole to use. A once-priest so enamoured with its sexual power that he had abandoned everything, even his immortal soul, for the promise of Asmodeus' touch.

I walked with my eyes closed. My bare feet pushed through the sand, my toes parting in the warmth. I opened my mind the same way I had once opened myself during prayer. Before, I'd hoped to be blessed with God's favour, but now I longed to be spoken to by another. I wanted Asmodeus to choose me, to see my plight as I offered my body to everything in my path. I hoped this would be enough to lead my way.

It was then that some new territory of Hell shivered into existence. The plains of nothingness were swept up in a storm. I had to shield my eyes against the grating sand. My cheeks were whipped raw, but I persevered, pressing forward through the wild winds in the direction I was drawn towards. Time passed before the storm lessened, and as my vision returned, I saw that the desert had transformed. I had wandered onto a rocky outcrop. In the dark distance, structures carved from a black rock loomed above me. A castle-like tower blocked out much light, and like tar, it seemed to drip down to the ground in an overlapping cascade of rough, thin rock. At the base, a sea of black stone rippled with sharp edges and glistening surfaces. I stood in awe, convinced I was before the vast expanse of a city, though unlike any I had ever seen.

I felt as if I had passed through numerous levels or planes of existence; some part of me knew intrinsically I had fallen deeper into Hell and that my fate here had been sealed. If everything before now had been a simple test, then what was next? Could I even comprehend it with my mortal mind?

Human fear bloomed in my chest. I shivered, though I was not cold. Like an animal, I cast my head about, and I felt the emptiness of my flesh—I craved a warm embrace or to be filled. I wanted some creature to come forth and prove to me that I was wanted and worth having. But at that moment, I was suddenly exposed. I feared my humanness would make me akin to a delicacy. I did not know the politics of Hell beyond what I had recently learned. Plenty of lesser demons could want to use me for their own purposes and could keep me from Asmodeus for eternity. And my desire to be at Asmodeus' side would be so obvious that, caught by the wrong conniving demon, I would be trapped here eternally, with Asmodeus just out of reach. Nothing could tell me if any of these creatures would entertain the bargain I had made with Asmodeus, even if it was the Prince of Lust and a King of Hell.

Walk, I commanded myself. *Remember your duty.*

A lifelong servant's natural inclination to order is to obey. I had been in service to the church since I was a boy, and all defiance had long ago been trained out of me. My body understood what to do by the order of my own mind, and I disengaged the human emotion, leaving it trailing behind in the sand to walk further into Hell. If I faced those pitfalls, I would deal with them as they came.

As I walked, the landscape changed ever so slightly. Everything still glowed a deep red, like the sunset had been sliced open and the very core of the sun had bled across the land. The outcrop sloped downwards, and as I slid over rock and landed on a path beneath, I realised I would be walking into the depths of this crowded onyx city. Though perhaps the word 'city' conjures the wrong image: there was little noise and bustle. I heard nothing in the way of animals or music. The most I could hear was an ambient drone, a sad noise dipping toward mourning. The closer I got, the less certain I became of the structures I had seen. From afar, what had appeared as a municipality made of an intricate web of stone might have merely been just that—stone without structure or meaning behind it. A random assortment or a natural occurrence. The light hitting at odd angles, or my human prejudice carving meaning out of nothing. And I believe this new world heard me, for my sight blurred, and I became so uncertain about what lay ahead of me that I had to stop walking altogether. All clarity darkened, a vignette in my eyes that tunnelled my focus. With the intensity of the black stone ahead, I suddenly could see no light.

No, I thought and stopped walking. *No, I do not like this.*

It was such an innocuous, human thought. It seemed smaller than the actual feeling enveloping me. *I do not like this* —I can almost laugh now, even though, at that moment, a great terror gripped my heart. I think what happened was this: my body became aware of its nature, its mortality, its life. It felt as if I wasn't meant to be there, and I cast my mind back desperately to the ritual I had committed to enter here. I *had* killed myself, had I not? I had stabbed myself with eager willingness—but perhaps what was happening was a delayed reaction. A spirit who could still feel his flesh. A spirit who was using it eagerly. I thought: *well, then what is happening to me is to be expected.* Despite everything, I was still human; I wanted clarity or certainty in a place that lacked either. The sudden fear that I wasn't actually dead engulfed me, and it felt worse than believing I had truly succumbed in that Cave of the Sibyl. My body was lying in my own blood and that of Bishop Favio—and my body was also here, experiencing pleasure it had never encountered in life.

I hadn't realised I had sat down until I heard the voices. When I peeled my head off from my knees, my location had shifted once again. Slumped in the dirt, back pressed against rock, and with only the great looming tower of black rock to orient myself, I had moved far to the east, so that the tower now sat to my left.

"What. . ." I wheezed.

Ahead of me was a worse sight. In a field of strange, prickly red flowers, several figures danced and whooped. They were dressed in cream-coloured sacks and were barefoot. Their faces were off-centre and drooping as if half melted. My chest seized at the sight of them, and I pressed back into the rock, unsure of myself or their friendliness. Their uncanny nature had me shivering—I knew they weren't human, though they seemed akin to my form. Two legs, two arms, a head of hair, though theirs ran in wet, stringy clumps from their scalp. Demons, or spirits and the like. Captivated, I ended up watching their work, which seemed to be little more than dancing and celebrating. They paid me no mind. Momentarily ghost-like, I could view all the secrets of their ceremony.

I did not question how I had moved. Distantly, I knew my human nature would be a bane here—I felt certain I would one day go insane if I could not reconcile my mortal mind with the impossibility of all I had experienced. But for now, I pushed upright, weight drooping as I clung to the rock for purchase.

"It is human," a voice said, croaking and ancient. I blinked and looked up.

All five figures were suddenly in reaching distance. Five faces—all of them slumped and dripping, skin in pulled layers drooping down—were peering at me. Their eyes were entirely black, both the whites and the iris drowned in ink-like colour. I screamed unashamedly. They moved with speed, cackling and dancing. Their long hair and their bodies looked like facsimiles of women—witches, hags, crones. I felt that's what they were, or what they were akin to. Four moved away and laughed and danced, but one lingered.

"Eat," it told me. It knelt down and reached its fingers forward. They were long, spindly things, with more knuckles than any human hand could possibly bear. The skin faded to a mottled grey so that the fingers themselves were shrivelled. The sight of them conjured the thought of mummification, and the nails were overly long and sharp. With odd gentleness, it plucked one of the flowers from the ground and held it out to me.

I—whimpered. It twisted the stem of the flower between forefinger and thumb. The bloom danced, spinning as the crones did. I focused on it.

Stretched red petals bounced with the movement. The

flower was unlike any I had seen, appearing elongated and deformed. It had filaments so long they tickled my nose, and with the flower so close to me, it resembled some massive insect, antennas scraping at my lips.

"Eat," the crone encouraged, and I seemed to have no preservation left in me. I enjoyed doing what I was told. Pathetically, I opened my mouth, and the creature pressed the bloom inside, nodding as I chewed.

Bitter flavour exploded on my tongue. The texture was soft and chewy, and I writhed as that awful, pervasive taste coated the inside of my mouth. I went to spit it out—and the creature was on me. It leapt up and pressed its hand over my mouth. I groaned and thrashed, but it was strong.

"Where art thou going?" the crone rasped. Gently, it scraped its long nails across my cheek and down onto my neck, where it massaged down my throat again and again until I swallowed.

I could feel the chewed flower as it slid down my throat, and I shivered in disgust, aware of its slow movement down my oesophagus. I thrashed again, and this time, the crone above me backed off. The creature, still on all fours, cocked its head and crept backwards until it was some distance from me.

Again, it asked, "Where art thou going?"

I did not know what to tell it. I worried it would keep me here with the rest of its fellows, preventing me from reaching my goal. But it was persistent. When I did not answer immediately, it croaked again, "Where art thou going?" and the rest of its brethren echoed the question whilst they danced and laughed.

I could have said Asmodeus, but I did not wish to reveal every secret of mine. I knew I must find one from each level of the hierarchy before I would come before Asmodeus, so I said, "I must find a President of Hell."

The dancing stopped. This seemed to give them pause.

"To Malphas thou go," a crone said. It pointed to its right, to my left—where the tower loomed in that grey distance, the red of the sun glowing violently at its back.

The distance baffled me. I coughed over a piece of that flower and sat up straighter. "How?" and then, immediately, "Will you take me?"

"We are not permitted to go there," the crone in front of me said.

I blinked and felt somehow more in tune with my flesh. Frowning, I pressed a hand against my stomach and shook my head—which caused no nausea and no confusion. As I peeled my palm away, I saw with great delight that the wound on it had completely healed. Stigmata free, my flesh reborn. The same went for my feet, which had only the bloody smear of the old wound to prove there had ever been one.

The crone nodded at me as if to say, "Yes, I helped you," and I did not know what to do with that knowledge. I had only my body to offer to thank it, and as much as I had told myself I did not mind what fucked me, these creatures disturbed me so wholly I wanted to rescind that statement.

"What did you feed me?" I whispered.

The crone pointed to another of the flowers it had pressed into my mouth. "Something of this plane, for thou to grow accustomed."

"Walk this road and call out to Malphas," another crone said. "Then they will come for thou."

They watched me with equal parts interest and neutrality. I felt I'd had enough of this place and pushed up finally.

"Thank you," I said, "for the flower."

And I was told, "Thou may not like what thou wilt become during thy stay here."

I SPENT MORE time walking and navigating along the road, which became little more than a tiny path on a standalone ridge. The cliff fell away until I was walking on top of a thin road on a sharp slope. To my right, nothing but opaque foggy clouds and the cries of the damned. To the left, that sleek black city, though it now appeared so deep and impossible to reach that I did not dare step off the path.

In the distance, the path curved, but the light and the fog made it impossible to see its end. So I walked, and I called out the name Malphas as I had been told, though the name felt unfamiliar to me. I did not know to whom—or what—I called.

"Malphas!" I cried out. My voice was wicked away from me by the expanse and the wind. The sounds of the damned drowned out my plead, and I tried to cry out with desire and joy more so than fear, as if I could lace my words with heat and the demon would hear me over tortured screams. "Malphas, I call to you! I summon you! I want you!" I cried.

But it wasn't wholly true. I wanted Asmodeus. I wanted to see the true form of the Prince of Lust, to revel in the horror of its demonic flesh, to be rendered its whore. And so when I next called to Malphas, I said, "I am Asmodeus' creature! But for this moment, I could be yours!"

As I said it, I was engulfed in cloud and fog. It dispersed slowly, and when it did, I could see that the path had abruptly stopped.

I halted before I cautiously crept closer to the edge. Stone crunched beneath my feet, and pebbles cascaded over the side. Nothing sat at the bottom of it except a descent into the depths of Hell, a pit of nothingness as far as my human eyes could ascertain. I glanced up. In the distance, covered by low-hanging clouds, the tower stood ominous and groaning. The wind whistled across the structure, whipping its façade, and the sound that echoed out sounded bat-like—a screeching that had me shivering.

I remembered my nakedness as Adam and Eve had, and the cold pelted down upon me. Shivering, I gripped myself and said, "Malphas, President of Hell! Hear my plea!"

Again, that screeching sounded and delayed the wind struck me. I almost lost my footing and slid in the grainy dirt.

I looked up at the tower. "Malphas!" I cried again, and then, from the shadowy distance, something emerged.

It took time for me to comprehend them. They appeared to be little more than amorphous blobs bobbing on the horizon. But as they got closer, they resolved.

Four creatures howled in mid-air, their stout bodies held aloft by leathery wings. Their back legs were goat-like, and their were arms small and useless. They had wild grins on their faces as they flew towards me, and I thought: *these are imps.*

I'll admit to being afraid. In the end, all I really wanted was a desperate, filling fuck. I would offer myself to Malphas gladly—but I did not want to be touched by these strange creatures. As they resolved and I saw what lay between their legs—thick members that leaked and twitched—my mind and my body revolted against one another. What happened in my stomach seemed to happen at the sight of any cock; an opening in the pit of my core, and my morals and my standards were gone. Clouded by arousal and desire, I was only half committed to running. But run I did. I turned with a gasp. Across that thin and dangerous path, feet slapping against the warm stone, I ran until my lungs burned.

But they were quicker than I could ever be. I heard their wings beating, the wind pounding in my ears, and as I half-turned to see my assailants, one dashed out at me.

The first one grabbed at my arm and lifted it high. The socket ached as it pulled against my shoulder, and I screamed, scrabbling to get away. Alone, the creature was strong enough to heft me just slightly off the ground. Its hands and feet were without claws, but the pressure of its grip still made my body ache; all my weight hung from my shoulder, and I feared it would pop out. When the other three joined the first imp in carrying me, I became weightless. They lifted me, and my feet kicked for purchase, meeting nothing but sharp, cool air. Every beat of their wings bobbed us closer to the tower, and I hoped this was a greeting party of sorts—that Malphas had heard me.

"Where are you taking me?" I shouted, but they did not reply to me. I was unsure if they could even speak. For minutes, I let myself be carried, arms outstretched in a pose echoing crucifixion, and when I asked again, "Where are you taking me?" one imp screeched in annoyance and walloped me on the head.

CHAPTER TWO

I woke on cold, black marble, in a room of cathedral arches and sprawling majesty. The only light burned from snarling braziers, and in the fog of wakefulness and low-light, I relied not on sight, but scent. A stench like sulphur and sex pervaded the room despite its high ceilings. As my eyes adjusted, I saw that my impish captors lingered in the rafts above as little more than stout, gargoyle-like shadows. They chittered occasionally to one another, but none made any attempts to swoop at me, not even when I pressed up on my knees and looked about.

I was bruised. Annoyed. I was as willing as any human could have hoped to be in this place, and my eagerness had yet to be rewarded. My nakedness felt so akin to vulnerability, and with the frigid marble biting my knees, the first creeping fog of regret began to edge into my mind.

The room itself was austere and inhuman. The far wall had clearly been made from the same stone I had seen in the distant city. It dripped sleek black down to the marble as if the stone had been melted and cooled like magma. Beneath this melting affair of stone, a cluster of jagged rocks gathered into something resembling a chair. A throne.

Then, shooting out from either side came semi-circle seating, a far distance up this great wall. From my low vantage, I could see no way to climb them. Vaguely, it resembled a courtroom, with these stands high up and out of reach. Or perhaps Rome's Colosseum, with an audience gathered to watch my bloody demise. As my eyes settled, I became aware of shadows in the seats, bright eyes watching me. More imps.

"What?" I croaked out. I sat pathetic and small with my hands covering my limp cock, feeling more alone than ever. The sound of my voice spooked the imps, who all began to roar. I shrunk back timidly, watching them jump and whoop in the stands. Above me, the four-winged imps who had carried me here dove down. They dashed forward towards the braziers and, one by one, lit the ends of their tails with fire. The scent of burning flesh filled my nostrils. Instinctively, my body curled in on itself. But they did not fly towards me.

Instead, they took position, forming a kind of circle in the air. Their tails dropped down like hanging lanterns and, from this new light, I could see something had been carved on the ground.

A sigil.

I was no master of the dark arts. I had fumbled my way into Hell, groping at my body and flesh. In the strange carving, I could only recognise the feeling in my gut whenever something occult occurred. My eyes burned. I clenched my fist. Old habits made my mouth run dry at the sight.

"What am I to do?"

My voice came out still hoarse. I wet my lips and asked the question again. Nothing was said, but from the dark stands, something whistled towards me. I flinched just as a dagger splintered the marble, its hilt wobbling from the force of the precise throw. My body moved to pick it up, but my mind was on Asmodeus; on the way I had drawn blood from myself that night, coated my cock with it, fucked up into the sticky palm of my hand chanting its name. *Come to me,* I had thought.

And now I was crawling to the Prince of Lust. But to get to it, I had to face this trial first.

I pushed my body forward and pressed my hand over the sigil, feeling the grooves beneath my fingertips. They were thankfully shallow, and as the imps waited for me, I picked up the dagger, raised my arm over the carving, and slit open the palm of my hand.

Barely any blood fell. I squeezed out the drops I could, and as I watched them fall, I thought: *this will take too long.* Add to this my humanness and the fact I could still feel pain, and my commitment began to waver in the long minutes it took for my blood to coat the sigil.

Then, hypnotic and deep, I heard the rumble of my new God in the depths of my mind, urging me onward.

Come to me, little priest. Prove your worth.

Emboldened by the voice of Asmodeus, I took the sharp dagger and dragged it over my forearm, splitting deep in the skin. Blood flowed more freely. I grit my teeth, bore it, and cried out, "Malphas, President of Hell! I summon thee! I want thee!"

The room hummed with approval. The imps stamped with their feet, and the room's structure shook, the very stone resonating and vibrating as if with glee. A light split through from the distant ceiling, so bright I had to shield my eyes against the onslaught, and raucous cheering went up around me. When the light finally faded, I peeled back my hand.

The black seat was now occupied.

There, half slumped in my own blood and sweat, with cold marble pressing against my body, I bore witness to Malphas for the first time.

The creature was unique. Humanoid in some respects and animalistic in others. Its head was that of a raven. An inky-blue down of feathers covered its neck and tickled the top of its chest, which became human in appearance, though its skin maintained a strange leather-like quality, the flesh glistening a deep midnight blue. For the parts of its body that were human, it was large and muscular—not as impressive as Asmodeus, of course, but more spectacular than any human male I had ever come across. My eyes raked down its body, which, even from the distance and the low light, stood out to me. If the demon itself was large—I guessed it would stand at about eight feet when it stood—my eager and salacious mind wanted to see whether other parts of it would be proportionate.

So, I looked.

I dropped my gaze to between its log-like thighs and saw the twitching bulge of its exposed cock. Perhaps the width of my forearm, as substantial as the cocks those two lesser demons had ravished me with. My heart pounded. I barely had to think, barely had to consider what it would feel like to have that pressing inside me before my own nether region stirred to life, heat gathering in a taut ball behind my stomach.

Fuck.

The room filled with ragged breathing, anticipation wet and dewy like morning mist. I did not move from my outstretched position, unsure of myself. *Should I get up? Should I bow to it?* My mind was so overrun with anxious questions that I became impotent, save, naturally, for my hardening cock.

When the demon exhaled, the room rumbled, and the imps practically screamed.

Its voice sounded gravely, low as if coated in dirt and mud. Every word it spoke was deliberately slow. "I am Malphas," it announced, "the mighty Great President of Hell, who commands forty legions of demons. Thou art mine summoner; thou has't called me to appear. For what purpose?"

Sound bled from the room. The imps were silent again. I could hear nothing save for the crackling of the braziers and the small flames still alight at the end of the flying imps' tails. Aside from this, I perfectly heard the sound of my frightened, anticipatory heart running in my chest. I pushed up and crawled forward until I had pulled my body over the bloody grooves of the sigil and could splay myself in genuflection at the demon's feet.

"Great Malphas," I said, fumbling for an epithet. "My prince has ordered me to go to it. Your King. I must prove myself to it."

Malphas seemed to look at me more carefully than before. Its raven-head cocked to the side, bird eyes blinking eerily. "How has't thou been charged to proveth thyself?"

I—froze. This felt somehow like a trap. Too frightened to meet its gaze, I said, "I am nothing, great Lord."

It chuckled then, very briefly, and the imps laughed with

it, abruptly cutting themselves off when Malphas grew silent. "Obviously," it said, voice stretching.

I swallowed. This wasn't right—not how I expected this to go. The feeling that I was somehow on trial consumed me, and the collective gaze of the imps became judgemental. I bowed my head lower and told it: "I gave up my earthly life to become Asmodeus' toy. I summoned it into my abbey and let it ruin me. It vanquished my love for God and my faith, and I could think of nothing else but the pleasure it brought, and so I entered Hell willingly. But I forgot myself. I forgot my place. To Asmodeus, I am just another body it might use for its pleasure, another mortal corrupted by its power. I wish to prove myself and to do so, I must climb the ranks. The lesser demons sent me on this path: to the Presidents, the Knights, the Earls, Marquises, Princes, and Dukes—before I get to the King of this circle, Asmodeus itself."

The raven-head Malphas opened its mouth, splitting the black beak in two. A snake-like tongue hissed out of its mouth as it said, darkly amused, "And dost thou wish me to fuck thee?"

The imps erupted into petulant, scalding laughter. I flinched from the sound—their screeching finger-pointing, their jeering, their stamping upon the stone. Even the four that had flown me in began to giggle and point. How. . .embarrassing.

I was a fool, to some extent. I had thought one dangerous fuck split over two demonic cocks would be enough to squash the root system of shame in my body. But these knots were convoluted, and even the pleasure I got from being used seemed not enough to stop me from feeling it. I thought of God. I thought of the bishops and the priests I had left behind and betrayed. I imagined what they were thinking of me now, how they might be damning my very memory for all I had done. My chest burned. I tried to resolve my expression and return to pious neutrality, but Malphas clapped its hands together, and the thunderous boom silenced everything.

Its throat bobbed as it talked. The sound that emerged was sluggish, each word fighting to reach my ears. "What petulant, vain thinking thee display," Malphas grumbled. "To think I, great Malphas, servant to the fallen angels, our demon lords, would'st e'er wish to sully myself by inserting my member into human filth. But neither am I able to betray the intentions o' the King Asmodeus, the Prince o' Lust, who ruleth the circle in which I live. I find myself at a great impasse," it said, "and I shall punish thee for it."

It was like lacerating a cyst. Anticipation had gathered in a hot, tight ball beneath the shared skin of us all, and Malphas' words struck at my very centre and split me apart. Punishment, however painful, promised pleasure. And for the demons here, all gathered to watch a show, my humiliation was all but guaranteed.

I craned up to meet Malphas' gaze. Unimpressed, eyes blank and uncaring, I saw no desire to have me in the raven-black stare. As if I was little more than an inconvenience, it made a gesture in the air.

Everything happened at once. First, the stands packed tightly with imps flared to life again. I could *feel* the quickening pulse of that mad crowd, and my own heart sped up to match it. Above me, the four imps squealed with glee. They broke from their formation and began to circle me, their tails whipping through the air and snuffing out their flames. A new darkness descended. My eyes had adjusted only slightly, so I could barely pick up any details from their bodies as they dashed down upon me.

Their small, firm hands tugged at my limbs. Each of the four took an arm or a leg and stretched me until I was helplessly splayed out, exposing my naked torso to the view of every one of the creatures in the stands and Malphas itself. It gave a low hum of approval. Even without words, my body instinctively understood praise. It was exhilarating. My body burned. Malphas spoke in some infernal language I couldn't comprehend, this quick barking order. The imps heeded the command instantly, and from this horizontal stretch they had pulled me into, they flew directly upright. Two let go of my legs and moved out of my periphery. Within seconds, I hung vertically from my arms, lower body dangling in the air. At this higher vantage, I overlooked the cheering stands of imps.

I locked eyes with the great President. Too much sound occurred; the delight of the imps came in shouts and cries, and my heart raced. I shivered in humiliation. But I could hear Malphas clearly when it spoke.

"I see what thee used to be. For e'ry degenerative act thou hast committed in this hellish pit, thy time in the cloth still clings to thee. I sense mine own brethren tried to fill thee withal their seed, if just to abate the stench o' godliness and purity thee surrounded thyself in for so long. But I can smell it still. Thou reeks."

I watched Malphas stand slowly. The creaking of its body echoed throughout the hall, muffled only faintly by the impish squall. As it stood and its body lengthened, I saw I had been right. It stood about seven feet tall, and it walked over to my suspended position with unblinking eyes.

"I can not let thee pass through mine own realm and into that o' the King Asmodeus withal thy past still wafting off thy flesh. And so I shall deposit upon thy skin and into thy orifice the seed o' many lesser demons, to weaken the stench. And though I shall not enter thee, I shall gift thee withal mine own seed, as it is the wish o' mine own Lord. In return, thou shalt scream and cry and beg for it. Thou shalt hark to what I know o' thy holy brethren; o' the things they desire. Thou shalt hark to this as mine own imps defile thee. Dost thou understand this?"

All the blood was rushing from my arms to my groin. Heat tugged together in my stomach, and my cock twitched in answer. "Yes," I said, somewhat breathlessly—though perhaps not truthfully. Listening to Malphas' dark knowings as I was defiled would be difficult. Had I really considered the actuality of the information it would share with me?

What did I fear if I learned the desires of Bishop Fazio, or Bishop Jonah, or the young and beautiful Oliviero, who, no doubt, had learned of my demise in the Cave of the Sibyl?

Two things came to mind. First, they knew of my real nature and what I had done to Bishop Fazio. This would only be possible if they had managed to roll away the blockage that had sealed mine and the bishop's body in the cave, and perhaps their faith in my goodness would allow them to craft some other fantasy that might override the grim reality. That a demon had caused it all to happen. That the cave was full of evil. That it was a mouth to Hell and all inside had occurred without the actions of a desperate whore—the locals already believed this, as Bishop Fazio had told me.

If this wasn't the true reason I felt fear, then only the second option remained: that others in the abbey harboured forbidden desires as obscene as my own, and I had squandered my time in two ways. I could have had them, and they could have had me.

I feared that not only had I waited too long, but I had waited for no good reason.

I shivered at the thought, and roughly, I was called back to the present moment by something pressing into my mouth.

I opened wide on instinct, but it was not Malphas' member nor that of an imp. As my vision cleared and my senses returned, I felt the long-nailed fingers of Malphas encompassing my head. Its hand was pressed against my face, and something had split from its palm—a long, fleshy thing that was pushing down my throat.

I gagged. My body revolted, spasming around the intrusion. Little air made it in. and as I writhed, kicking the air weakly, with Malphas' body too far for me to reach, I thought: *am I dying?*

"Ah, those hags discovered thee," Malphas said. Whatever part of its body was in my throat writhed, and I groaned, choking pathetically around it. The saliva in my mouth began to spill from my lips. "Thou hast eaten from mine own realm."

Oh-I tried to speak. Indistinct and muffled sound spilled wetly from my throat. Malphas hushed me and cupped my face with a gentle touch.

"'tis not this I shall punish thee for, for the act o' indulgence is not sinful. Nought thee could do in the way o' desire is worthy o' punishment in this place. But now that thou hast eaten and thy mortal flesh is settled, thou art one o' Hell's creatures. There is no turning back for thou. I must rid thee o' thy priestly scent all the more."

Then, roughly, it pulled its flesh out of me. Thick, stringy saliva fell from my mouth. My throat was raw, and when I gasped, the air felt scalding against the scraped internal flesh. Malphas made a noise like a low chuckle and patted my cheek, though not gently. Coughing, I gasped for air again. "What—what was that?"

I watched as something resembling a meaty tube retreated into Malphas' palm, which sported a gaping human-like mouth. The skin of the palm puckered around it, forming makeshift lips, and it was toothless. But the tube, with its wet opening, slid slickly back into the gash. I whimpered. Malphas groaned at whatever look took over my face and gripped my chin hard.

"These imps are lesser demons in many ways, little

human," it rumbled. The cheers in the stand took on a new kind of sound, a fretful, eager noise—whooping, a clicking of tongues that sounded faintly like animals scratching at doors. Malphas said, "Where many named denizens o' Hell wert servants and followers o' the angels who fell, imps themselves wert born in Hell itself. Their minds are made entirely o' sin. They do best withal orders, withal encouragement, near mindless is their existence. And so I have given them an order."

Without further explanation, it stepped back and returned to its earlier position, sinking that thick, resplendent body into the stone chair, and in the low light, its skin glinted like black opal, and I could see God's make in its body. I could see how it had once been a servant of Heaven and how its form would have frightened any normal mortal, and more than that, I understood implicitly how insignificant humanity was. The muscular arms and legs of Malpahs spread, and its thick cock grew hard. Its black eyes remained open, deep tar pits that flowed out to me, glinting like the night sky.

"Prove thyself," Malphas commanded.

And the imps descended.

3

CHAPTER THREE

I knew how foolish it would be to stiffen or fight or resist. And yet, if a part of me wanted this, another part filled with fear. My eyes dashed to the rows upon rows of cheering imps, but not one of them flung themselves from the stands to get to me. Instead, they came from above.

I flinched away on instinct, anticipating pain. But instead, three of the four imps began to touch my body and hold me upright in the air as they did. Simple touches, fingers pressing over my nipples and down my belly. Another dragged its digits in gentle strokes over my thighs and the last up my back. All tension bled from me. I drooped into the touch, shivering as small pleasure buzzed throughout my body. Against the firm grip of the final imp who held my arms above me, I let all my weight go, giving up on fighting this limp position. My fingers began to tingle as the blood drained from them, and my head felt lighter as a mix of pleasure and discomfort began to cloud my judgement.

Quickly, I realised I was on display. Part of me had considered this a trial, but another saw this as entertainment. The waiting imps cheered in the stalls, infernal language spilling from their pinched mouths, eagerness clear as they shook and cried out.

For some reason, defiance bubbled up in me. For all my talk about understanding my place, how I intrinsically knew the worthlessness of my body and my desire, the thought that I was above these imps was inevitable. I wanted to be sinking down onto Malphas' cock, used as a one-time toy and discarded when the demon had finished with me. Instead, I would be used by freakish creatures without names nor status in this place. I reached a new level of shame, made all the worse by the pleasure they were giving me.

One imp latched down upon a nipple. I cried out, unused to the sudden pleasure—it was as if a direct line existed between that pink nipple and my cock, and every time that thin tongue licked out and sucked and nipped, a flooding sensation engulfed my lower half. Its fingers moved deftly to the other nipple, and it was pulled, tugged, twisted. My sensitivity had me crying out, and the noise attracted the laughter and whooping of my audience. I squeezed my eyes shut. The darkness made it easier to withstand the flushing heat in my cheeks, but it only intensified the feeling of what the creature was doing to my nipples.

Then, the imp holding my arms dropped one, and I sank somewhat in the air, arm slapping unceremoniously against my thigh. It regained its grip on my left arm and took up several little fistfuls of my hair, which it then used to hang me from. Like that, head back and neck strained, I dangled. The pressure on my scalp was not quite pain—I felt like a cat held by the nape, made impotent. A moan escaped my throat, and that was it: my sound acted as a signal for the imps to act. The other two imps cackled, a noise that echoed in the crowded audience. The two imps dragged their stout, thick cocks over my body. The one that had latched onto my nipples stopped, dragging itself up so it could rub the weeping head of its own across one of my hard, pink nubs. The one holding me up shimmied lower and pulled my head back with its hands. Against my face, it slapped its purplish member. I stuck my tongue out, and a wet sound echoed out as my breathing grew heavy. It ploughed its fingers through my hair and made a satisfied grunt of its own. My one free hand was taken up by another imp and guided to its cock, and the other one put its mouth on my swollen, twitching member, grinding itself down on my thigh. My mind vacated.

The imp above me pressed into my mouth and began to thrust shallowly. Instinct took over. I felt no shame, then, and no fear of what I had become. I felt at peace in my body and my soul; I felt delectable, saintly in an unholy way, inspired by some higher power, and reduced to a slut. I sucked dutifully at the head, tongue licking out to lap at the leaking precum. I pooled as much saliva into my mouth as I could manage, a mouth already made soaking by whatever Malphas had placed in me, and my jaw worked sloppily around the thrusting motion of the imp's cock, which pulsed and throbbed in my mouth.

It played with the angle of my head, moving this way and that, pushing in as far as it could go until it hit the back of my throat. I gagged and spluttered, and in response, it made disappointed, aggravated noises until, finally, it found the position that opened my throat into a straight channel. When it sank into me, I forgot how to breathe. The cock was so wide it clogged up the passage of my throat, and I had to push against it with my tongue to gasp a slither of air into my lungs.

My grip around the other imp's cock slackened, and in anger, it beat at my body. Sudden pain had me thrashing. I kicked the air, screaming and whimpering as I was choked by the thing in my throat. I squeezed my hand firmly around the throbbing imp and it started snapping its hips up in earnest, thrusting and grinding, with its hands pressed down upon mine to encourage me along. The third imp, which had begun to lick and play at my poor, bloated cock, sucked lightly at the blushing tip. Tendrils of teasing pleasure sparked throughout my core, and my eyes rolled back into my head just as the imp in my throat began to fuck with immaculate devotion.

It was an onslaught. I was gagging. Tears sprang to my eyes, and I could think of nothing except a quiet prayer not to throw up. Part of me revolted; there was an instinct to run away, but I had never been so hard, never had such wetness leaking from my swollen tip—every thrust of my hips was a confirmation of my unholy, worthless nature. The other imps and what they wanted fell away as the imp above me lowered itself even further, so far down my throat I could barely gag. Its balls pressed against my open mouth, resting on my teeth, jaw made so wide it began to ache, and like that, poised to shoot its cum directly into my stomach, it raised and lowered itself over and over into my throat.

Just as I thought it was about to cum, another cock began to push into my throat. It could barely fit, so full I was with the first imp—but this did not stop the other from trying. What little gap I managed to make to keep breathing was roughly plugged up by the tip of this new member. I blinked back tears, moan of protest muffled by the satisfied grunt of this new imp—the one whose cock I had long ago stopped rubbing. It had decided to prioritise its own pleasure.

The imp that had been licking at my cock sank down more fully, and from behind I felt, impish hands moving my ass cheeks apart. This imp reached around to fumble with my nipples, its tip prodding at my opening. As if all their minds were connected, the imps decided at once to move together. And so it happened like this: the imp at my ass pushed inside without preparation and without much in the way of lubrication. Violent, sharp pain split through my backside. I jerked unnaturally away from it, one free hand snapping back to try and push the imp out of me. But it grabbed the arm and held it back at that awkward angle, using it as leverage to drag its full length out of me and then rebound back inside. It took little time for the hole to relax and welcome the fucking. With the other imp at my cock, working diligently to lick and suck, and the two cocks moving in my throat, I was sent into a breathless, reeling daze.

The five of us were panting. As the imps pressed deeper into my throat, I choked and gurgled, eyes rolling to the back of my skull as I withstood the barrage of their thrusts. They took what they wanted from me, using the wet channel even as I began to suffocate. Weakly, I began to shake my head, pushing weakly at their small bodies above me, and in answer, one leaned down and wrapped its hands around my throat; crushing pressure, I couldn't breathe, and their cocks glided over the sphincter of my throat again and again. My stomach hurled.

I vomited. Head back, throat being used—the vomit had nowhere to go. Both imps moaned at the sudden new warmth, and my mouth flooded with new saliva. Throat obstructed, neck choked, and every thrust like a ruthless use of a toy, it was only a few seconds before my vision began to explode with stars.

Panic had me thrashing. I rocked my head from side to side as if trying to shake them loose. Pathetic. They could have used me all they liked, and I would have been powerless to stop it—because that was all I was in the end. A slut to be used. Had I forgotten that so soon?

The panic gave way to a kind of splintered consciousness,

a flashing of thought and feeling and fear and pleasure. I came weakly, coerced by the sucking pressure of the imp at my cock, and as that orgasm throbbed through me, so did my vision pulse away until darkness came.

I fell unconscious.

4

CHAPTER FOUR

I heard the chanting of learned men, as familiar to me as my own skin, and when I woke, I was not in Hell but in the chapel of the abbey, on my knees in prayer.

Unpleasant and excessive incense had become a haze in the air. Inhaling it triggered a bodily response in me. I shivered, fearful that what had happened to me in Hell was little more than a dream.

"No," I mumbled.

"*Shh*." A biting twist of a sound. I looked up and saw Don Santi, one of my fellow dons, glaring at me. He shook his head in disapproval of my disrespect, but beside me, a comforting hand reached out and pressed against my back.

"Do not worry about him," a young man said. "He is simply jealous."

"What?" I half turned my head. Confusion bludgeoned me, for it was none other than Oliviero, looking much as he had the last time I had seen him. He smiled at me and rubbed my back comfortingly, and the motion was somewhat more intimate than I recalled him ever being with me. My mind, already so thoroughly dirtied and impure, and my body, which until moments earlier had been being ravished by a quartet of imps, wondered how Oliviero might fare in Hell. If he would be like me, a slut on his knees, begging to be used. And as these thoughts coalesced, Olivero moved his hands. They slid delicately from my back to the front of my chest. He pressed his body close, intimate, breath huffing in my ear and warming my neck. When his tongue licked up the exposed skin there, I shivered and made a noise of protest.

"Hush," he told me. More confidence lay in that single word than I had ever heard in our years together. "I know you want me to. I know you always have. I suspected the rumours about your inclinations were true early on, and every stolen glance, every time you pulled your gaze away from me with fretful speed—it felt good, Alessandro, to be the object of your desire."

I breathed out hard. "I don't—"

"You don't need to pretend with me," he said. The foggy wall of incense cleared, and the pew we were in widened. All other people vanished as if wicked away by the smoke. It was just the two of us in this small chapel, both of us clad in simple black cassocks. Even as he thumbed at my chest over this fabric, it felt more sinful than anything I had done in Hell. I rocked forward, hands coming to rest on the pew in front of me, and Oliviero's hands lowered as he himself sank onto the ground.

I turned to face him. He genuflected, threw the sign of the cross quickly about himself, as if I was the altar. My body grew hot with the thought—that to these demons, to anyone who wanted, I would make an altar of my flesh, where every act of coupling and deviance transformed into worship.

Then, he pushed himself up and against my lips.

The kiss was gentle at first. Our lips landed clumsily on

one another. I got the sense that Oliviero had never kissed anyone, or at least had never had the practice, and the sense of his innocence shivered through me even though he was twenty-something. My stomach trembled. *More*, I thought. *More*. He heard me, somehow, because he moved his body closer and his mouth wider. His tongue felt warm as it licked at mine, the pressure soft, both of us breathing in deeply through our noses, sucking incense and each other's scents into our lungs. Oliviero's hands ghosted along my jaw, tentative touches. He kept pulling away and laughing breathlessly, the sound boyish and giddy.

"Turn the other cheek," he breathed, lips spreading into a smile against my face as I craned away from him, laughing with him at the absurd and ill-placed reference. But I was not thinking of scripture, then. Not when his lips pressed against my neck, not when he gripped at the pleats of my cassock with such intensity I thought he might tear the thing off me. Oliviero's arms wrapped around me, and I—hesitated.

He pulled away. His face closed off and grew impenetrable. "What is it?" he asked without concern.

It was as if a part of me was fighting the fantasy. I don't know—I had had Bishop Jonah's cock down my throat, knowing distantly it was demonic fancy. I knew again that this was not the young man I had left at the abbey, sun blooming across his pale skin. Part of me found this to be a regression, a return to something I had thought I'd overcome. All the lust that had fermented inside me over years and years had been extracted by the first nameless demons I had met in Hell. So what was Malphas doing by sending me back here? What delicious new torture did it intend me to endure?

Oliviero's face swam into view, a thing of beauty. With heavy, lust-filled eyes, both his hands pressed into my cheek. He leaned forward again to kiss me firmly. The firm press of his stubble bit into my skin. Then he pushed more firmly into me, and I felt the swell of him beneath his cassock. He pressed it against my own firm member, and he looked up shyly, both hands still cupping my cheeks.

"Alessandro," he whispered. "Does it matter why this is happening? Don't you want me? Don't you want to taste me?"

I grabbed him, crushing his lips against mine. He moaned, chest expanding and shivering. I ran my fingers through his hair and let them tangle in the golden nest. I drank him like communion wine, each swallow a covenant made. Every wound I had ever endured, every heartbreak, every night I had laid awake cursing my own nature, begging God to let me die peacefully in my sleep—I forgot all those moments. I forgot everything except pleasure and the pursuit of it. This wasn't real; this was a demon's trick, a memory that had never happened. I embraced it as if it were a gift.

I pulled back from Oliviero, hands cupping his face. Something about his youthfulness roused a different part of me. I felt perhaps as the demons felt towards me: an urge to have him, to use him, to love him. My usual desire to sink onto my knees faded. I wanted *him* down there, craning up at me.

"Pray," I told him, and he knew what to do. He sank onto his knees with grace, his hands clasped and mouth moving. He took my order seriously, though I did not catch what prayer he spoke. Fragments of Latin slipped off his tongue. His voice, musical and full, was a whisper that was echoed by the stone surrounding us. I slipped my fingers into his hair and looked up to the vaulted ceiling, where stone angels and saints murmured back to us. I saw their carved lips moving in time with Oliviero and felt no fear at the sight.

He began to speak louder. His prayer crystallised.

"Sancte Michael Archangele," he said, eyes pressed together,

and I laughed. Laughed at the choice this version of Oliviero had made—a prayer to defend holy servants in battle, to protect against the Devil. *"Defende nos in proelio, contra nequitiam et insidias diaboli esto praesidium."*

Defend us in battle; be our defence against the wickedness and snares of the Devil.

"Oliviero," I murmured. He did not stop. At that moment, Oliviero was exactly as I remembered him. Devout to the point of deafness, I knew I was not there for him. So I watched him. I allowed myself the indulgent appraisal. His hair curled over his forehead. His lips were pinkish and lightly chapped; I ran my thumb over them.

"Imperet illi Deus, supplices deprecamur: tuque, Princeps militiae coelestis, Satanam aliosque spiritus malignos, qui ad perditionem animarum pervagantur in mundo, divina virtute, in infernum detrude."

May God rebuke him, we humbly pray. And do thou, O prince of the heavenly host, by the power of God, cast into Hell Satan and all the evil spirits who prowl about the world for the ruin of souls.

I reached down, forefinger gentle beneath his chin as I encouraged him to look up at me. Those wide eyes blinked at me; his mouth parted.

"Finish," I whispered.

He visibly swallowed, the bump in his throat gliding up. Peril and anticipation sat between us. This moment stretched. He brought himself to murmur, "Amen," and it felt as if he was concluding something more than his prayer, the way I had revoked my faith.

"I think my soul is already ruined," I told him, not caring if I was speaking to Malphas or to myself. I spoke to him as if he really were Oliviero and took my other hand to pat him, stoking his hair. "I think I have always been this way. That this moment was inevitable."

It was the truth. Many times, I had thought about my nature. Plenty of nights and prayers had been wasted on what I was and my eagerness to divorce myself from my desires. I had craved rescue, a religious intervention; I had played my entire life out in my mind again and again. If I had not stolen as a young boy, I would never have met God. Would the same crippling shame have threaded into my bones? Would I have been able to shack the fear of Him watching me? Would I have ever wasted so much time on a holiness and a goodness I would never achieve?

Failing that, if I had told Bishop Jonah what I was, would God have intervened then? If I had been truthful about my desires, would they have helped me?

The more I thought about it, the less certain I could be that any aid would have come. Slowly, like the setting of the sun, the knowledge settled in my stomach, not in the way of shameful inevitability but instead, a certainty. Like truth. My desires were ceaseless because they were natural. It would not have mattered if things had been different: I felt I would have always ended up here. Again and again, I would have walked into Hell, one way or another, embracing the truth of who I am.

Oliviero whispered, "Let he who is without sin," and he slipped his warm hand between the folds of my cassock. That soft palm of his wrapped around me. Instantly, I became light-headed, my vision woozy with delicious desire. He was economical with his motions, barely undressing me, moving the cassock aside so my cock slipped through.

"Oliviero," I breathed suddenly. I glanced down as that angelic face craned up at me, beautiful in its flushed state. He looked like a plum ripe for eating. The way my cock pressed against the soft skin of his youthful cheeks, the way his eyes were heavy with lust and distant with pleasure; it took everything in me not to press hungrily into his mouth. This—what the imps had done to me, what the demon resembling Bishop Jonah had done to me, and Asmodeus itself—I had never done. The demons who had taken me in their mouths did not count. Never had I had a young man on his knees eager to give me pleasure, and it frightened me how much I wanted it from Oliviero.

I—was a slut. If Oliviero had forced me down to take his cock, I would have done it without question. I grew eager with a new possibility: that my pleasure could be met in various ways, and the whoring of myself to demons could also involve stolen moments like this, where my pleasure became briefly central. This was no doubt a fantasy conjured by the demon Malphas. It had promised it would have me listen to the desires of my fellow priests. Though I doubted this was Oliviero's fantasy—I had wanted to send that man into ruinous deviance for years. I wanted to know what he looked like with my seed dripping over his face, with him rapidly blinking cum from his eyes.

Oliviero rubbed his cheeks against me. His lips only ever faintly ghosted over my twitching cock, and never for long. My grip in his hair tightened; it felt excruciating, this teasing. What was worse was when he moved his hand to curl in the rosary hanging by my side. He wrapped its beads around his hand and half around my cock. With slow, gentle movements, he dragged his hands up and down the shaft, the warm wooden beads rolling and pressing into the sensitive skin. I gasped and closed my eyes, focusing instead on the strange pleasure that came with the added texture. Then I heard wood against teeth, a precise clacking, and then wet moans. My eyes flittered open.

There Oliviero was, sucking the cross at the end of my rosary into his mouth. I watched it roll over his tongue and beneath it. I watched it disappear into the red, wet warmth of his mouth. I imagined untying the rosary and dipping the whole thing down his throat until he gagged and choked on the Lord's symbol—and it was this vision that made me grab his chin hungrily and tug him forward.

"You *whore*," I whispered. Oliviero opened his mouth with a breathy exhale, and the painted cross slipped over his lips, glistening with his saliva. I took my cock and patted Oliviero's whore cheek with it. He let out a small moan, and I pressed the head against his lips and then beneath them, running the tip around his gums. A tantalising taste of what his mouth would feel like. I squeezed my fingers around the base of my cock, imagining it to be the sphincter of Oliviero's throat. I imagined how he might whimper, the moans of protest as he gagged.

"*Fuck.*"

I did not ask. I told him, "Open," and he obeyed. That wet pink tongue of his lolled out of his mouth with a small noise, and he positioned himself with both arms in front of him so he resembled an eager, panting dog.

I glided over his tongue and into the wet embrace of his mouth. Oliviero moaned as I did, and a holy chorus sung in the rafters of the chapel, a *hallelujah* sang by stone angels. It was a new type of pleasure for me. Usually, when the urge hit, I could feel how empty my body was. But this? The warmth and the wetness, the eager sucking, the way his lips closed like a vice around me. I let him suck and tease for minutes, his pace odd and unrhythmic—but it didn't matter. I was close from the instant I sank into him, and this teasing stopped the mounting pleasure from building to a climax. He licked around the tip, tongue flat as he dragged it over the head.

"You've done this before," I whispered.

He moaned his agreement, and I pulled myself out of him. Oliviero groaned and rutted into the palm of his hand over his clothes.

"Tell me."

"Yes," he admitted, nodding. His hands reached for me, and I stopped him, holding my cock away.

His eyes glinted. "Whenever the Bishop wants me."

I imagined him between Bishop Jonah's legs, as I had been; I imagined him cramped into a confessional booth as the bishop listened to confession. I imagined the bishop in prayer and Oliviero sucking dutifully on his knees. I imagined him splayed on the altar, cassock bunched up around his neck, ass exposed as the bishop fucked into him—God, the thought enraged me and allured me at once.

Oliviero was *my* fantasy. I gripped his chin and forced my thumb to leverage his teeth apart. Then I plunged into the warm, wet hole of his throat. He craned back and moaned loudly. Ruthlessly, I surged again and again into his throat, and I did not stop even as he cried out and gagged and tapped at me for mercy.

I made a rat's nest of his beautiful hair, tangling my fingers in for grip. His saliva dripped onto the floor and formed a puddle his hand kept slipping in. Our moans matched, and he was *good*—a *good* boy. He sucked and bobbed his head even as it became too much for him. My legs began to shake from the angle I thrust in, and Oliviero wrapped his arms around them, squeezing them in comfort, his moans slipping more and more towards a pleading sound.

I was close. I slipped out of him. I wanted to see it spread over his face, dripping from his lips.

"Beg for it," I hissed.

"Please," he said, hand desperately moving his own cassock aside to reveal his own swollen pink cock. It was so wet with leaking precum that it looked painful. "Please, Alessandro."

I touched myself in earnest, and he met my pace, the both of us staring into each other's eyes. The chapel filled with the

sound of our wet hands and heavy breathing and the faint
sound of our angel audience, and then, as it built and built,
pleasure coalescing behind my belly button, pulling taut, the
closer I got—

"How doth it feel to know that many of thy holy brethren
could have been corrupted as thou wert?"

CHAPTER FIVE

Abruptly, the scene changed. My hands were pulled roughly above my head a moment before my orgasm, and my cock pulsed and jumped quite desperately. I thrust into the air, frustrated to the point of tears, barely registering the words that had been spoken to me or the fact both Oliviero and the chapel had disappeared.

I was back before Malphas. I was on my knees, with my hands pulled up and away from my body. Cum—not my own —had pooled around me. I wondered distantly if the imps had kept using me whilst I slept, a thought that made my untouched member pulse once more.

"Please," I said. My voice cracked. I could not hide how pathetic I felt, how desperate. At that moment, all I wanted was to cum. A heaviness clouded my mind; a warm dizziness overtook me. I ground my hips towards nothing and felt nothing but the air; no friction to aid me. My skin felt too warm. I needed—

Malphas spoke over my piteous begging. "That thou mightst have infected all of those folk with thy lust, and hadst those folk ravish thee f'r years and years in the house of God? Doth it upset thee?"

I found I was crying out of frustration. I thrashed against who or whatever was holding me. "Give me release!" I begged.

A great force slapped across my face, and my head slammed to the side. A bright and vicious pain throbbed over my cheek; I felt the answering dribble of precum leak from my swollen head. I whimpered, but the sound evoked no empathy from any of my watchers.

"Answer me, filthy mortal!" Malphas rumbled. The room filled with his rage, and my whole body quivered.

"*Yes!*"

My confession rebounded off the stone, and the imps in the stands cheered and whooped before Malphas raised his foot and stomped onto the ground. Another earthquake of a sound rolled percussive through the room.

The silence that descended after felt heavy. The eeriness, which came from the thousand sets of eyes resting on me and nothing but the distant creaking wind to listen to, had me shivering and uncertain. Malphas waited. I knew it wanted me to speak.

Be honest with yourself, I thought, because lying was the Church's business.

"If that was the truth," I whispered, "or in any way close to the truth. . .If any one of my brethren had even *thought* something similar to what I had. . .or perhaps indulged enough to touch themselves. Even if it was *women* they craved to the same extent as I craved men—"

I cut myself off, for I did not know how to end the thought. What would I have done? I might have felt less alone to know it, but the knowledge would not have been enough to keep me devout.

"What has't thee come to realise?" Malphas asked.

I exhaled shakily. "That. . . what I wanted and what I craved would never have been welcome in that place. That no matter who shared my desires, I would only have ever been able to indulge in them in secret. That what I want. . ." I breathed deep, inhaling sulphur, taking Hell into my lungs, "is this. Is you. Is Asmodeus. I want to belong to Hell; I want you to make an altar of flesh. I want to worship with my body. Please—let me *finish*."

Malphas' voice rumbled low and satisfied. "Well done, piteous human. Thee may has't thy recompense."

The imps who were holding my arms shifted so they were pulling them directly back. I rocked forward onto my knees, my back straight and ass raised. More like a dog than ever before.

Fingers appeared in my mouth, a set of impish, sharp nailed digits that pulsed in and out. I sucked them, tasting dirt and cum and other things I could not name, and once they had slicked their fingers up, they slipped out of my mouth with a pop.

Those same fingers were brought to my ass. The hole had already loosened. I guessed once more they had been using me for however long I had been in the fantasy with Oliviero —nothing but a receptacle for their fluids, a toy for their pleasure. *God*, the thought had me arching back.

Impish fingers sank into me. The feeling somehow moved deeper than their tips; I felt my insides pulse, the pleasure called forth from the intestinal maze. And then the fingers were removed and replaced almost instantly with a cock, and then another, pulsing in and out of me at different rhythms.

I became ruttish.

"*Ah, ah, ah!*" I met every thrust with a moan, and I tried to thrust back myself, eager to be fucked. I wanted to reach down and touch myself, but they still held my arms locked behind me. It meant every one of their thrusts rebounded through my body. As every one of their thrusts slid out, I jerked back the instant the sphincter closed around their tip, and I was brought sliding back down to the base of their cocks by the force of their hips.

Minutes went on like that. I was open-mouthed and drooling, my body fully on display, cock jumping between my legs with every bounce. The imps in the stands were back to applause, but I could barely hear anything, so fogged was my mind with pleasure.

Then, the imps began to fuck me forward. I was forced to crawl, every thrust moving me closer to the throne, where Malphas watched impassively. I could see its cock twitching at the sight of me, but it was not hard—and I knew intrinsically it would not renege on its promise to not fuck me. What, then, were the imps doing?

The cold marble floor dug into my knees, and every push forward sent aches up my thighs. Then, all at once, I was craning up to this raven-headed demon, completely at its mercy. Up close, I could not pretend to ignore the size of it. When it shifted, the sight caused me to cry out—a delirious sound that only enticed the imps to fuck faster and harder into my gaping hole.

"What—" I began, before impish fingers found their way into my mouth again. Two sets of hands held my mouth open, pulling back so I could only moan, not speak. Silenced like a whore, I watched fearfully as Malphas shifted. It brought its foot up—

—and pressed it against my cock.

Friction. Blissful, sudden friction. Next to the demon's enormous foot, my cock was barely noticeable. My pale skin pulsed and rutted up against its jet-black flesh. With near careless energy, it rubbed my poor swollen cock, bringing its pace in line with the imps, who fucked tirelessly into me, and it was about then that I lost time—or lost the ability to register much else except pleasure.

I could not tell you if anything else happened. My eyes rolled to the back of my skull and my body reached a point of luscious, indescribable feeling. Warmth, pleasure, an ecstasy that jolted my soul from the flesh itself, or an ecstasy that rendered my soul to nothing but my body—I couldn't be sure, except that when the orgasm came, it was nearly violent.

I cried out, my voice screaming through the air, and I kept thrusting up against Malphas' foot long after the initial shock had plundered me. Even as it began to ache, the feeling too much, too overwhelming, I kept rutting. I don't know how long I moaned and thrust forward. I don't know how long I kept moving.

All I know is, by the time I had recovered, and throes of pleasure had ebbed away enough for me to regain a sense of stability and consciousness, all the imps had disappeared.

I could still feel the ache in my body, the way my hole throbbed around nothingness, open to the world. My cock lay flaccid and spent over my thigh, and above me, Malphas watched as if it had never moved.

Malphas said, "Thee has't proven yourself, as mine own L'rd commanded of me. Thee art worthy of becoming a play-thing f'r the Prince himself. Wend on, dram lamb, blasphe-mous priest. Alloweth yourself be fucked again and again until Asmodeus opens his door to thee."

And like that, a door appeared. I turned, still splayed on the ground, as stone rumbled and between the black cliff spawned a slither of light. It was my passage forward.

When I turned back to Malphas, the demon was gone.

❧ 6 ❧
CHAPTER SIX

I n the tenebrous dark of that place, I let myself recover. For minutes, my mind felt apart from my body, still spinning above the vessel of my flesh with pleasure.

When it finally settled back into me, I found it difficult to move. My body ached with overuse, and as I pushed up, hand sliding in the wet mess pooling on the stone, my arm shook with the effort.

Sitting upright only made the exhaustion more obvious. Gravity urged me back down, and I had to fight the desire to sleep. I did not know how long the door would remain open, and so I hastily pushed myself up and began the walk over to it.

My feet, wet with fluids, slapped awkwardly along the stone. Wind blew through the tower, and I shivered in the cold breeze of it, mind still fogged with lush pleasure. In this sense, very few thoughts formed in my head—nothing coherent, nothing that said, 'Go here' or 'Do this'. I simply found myself pressing the palms of my hands against the jagged black stone, gliding my skin over the uneven texture beneath. It reminded me of the Cave of the Sibyl in some respect, namely the dank scent, thick with old, undisturbed earth and wet soil. My hands came away slightly damp, too, as something akin to water glistened over the walls.

The passage was barely wide enough for me to walk down front on. I would have to turn to the side and shimmy through it. If it weren't for the light at the end, which glowed a warm and inviting orange, I might have been scared—but I was beyond that feeling surely.

I turned my body and pushed down that toothed corridor. The instant my body was inside, the end I had entered from rumbled closed, and the resounding boom throbbed down my body and through the cramped space. My breathing went erratic instantly—not out of any conscious fear, but like a response from my body, which cowered at the mounting pressure building in my chest and lungs and the ever-present fear that I would somehow be crushed.

Do not be foolish, I thought, but that did nothing to relax me. In times like this, in the past, I would have prayed. My tongue went thick with that knowledge. I had no other way to cope, no practised method, and no knowledge of how to centre myself without the presence of God. And so I fell into old habits, with a new subject to laud.

Asmodeus, I thought. I prayed. *I come to you. Protect me.*

There was no answer. My heart sank, most likely because the demon had answered before. God never had, of course, but knowing Asmodeus *could* hear me, *could* reply, and for whatever reason chose not to—it made my heart hurt.

I kept moving, squeezing down that stone passage. The skin on my stomach and upper back gave way, sliced open by stone shaped at odd angles. I barely registered the pain, but warm blood ran in thin trickles down my body, my spine, my thigh; a terrible lubricant that did little to make the journey any slicker for me. All the while, I was coaxed towards the other end by that inviting warm light.

Come to me.

I heard Asmodeus, then, faintly. Like a cautious whisper carried by the wind, like it didn't quite want to say it, *come to me*, sounding more like a desire than an order for me to fulfil. I stopped in the cramped tunnel and closed my eyes, inhaling deeply that scent of petrichor and depth.

Soon, I told my prince. *I will be there soon.* In my mind's eye, I conjured that hierarchy the lesser demons had spoken to me about. I had passed the trials of the President of Hell, and so next was the Knight of this realm. I waited tensely for some kind of approval, some kind of acknowledgement, but nothing came. When I opened my eyes, I had to wonder if I had heard Asmodeus at all or just the whisper of my desperation echoing in my head.

I pressed on. For minutes, I pushed and scraped my naked body through the passage, and finally, when I reached the end and was roughly expelled out the other side, I breathed as deeply as I could and half collapsed onto the ground.

My fingers sank into warm, dry soil. I spent a minute deliberately not looking anywhere but my hands, at the way my fingers pressed and disappeared beneath the particles. The earth smelled fresh and upturned and *green* the way much of Italy did in the summer. I shivered and gained the strength to look up.

This part of Asmodeus' domain stretched to the horizon, an open plain dotted with dry brush tinged red as if stained by blood. I felt like I might run for hours and never reach the end of the field; in fact, I felt certain that would be what happened. The red sun and that impassable expanse of fields would drive me mad. Almost stubbornly, I stayed rooted to the ground, where my hands and bare feet could sink into the grassless soil, and I could be sure I was touching solid ground. Something about the way the grass swayed made me dizzy like it was an ocean stretching before me, not grass.

Like that, dog-like on all fours, I moved sideways, hoping to get a better lay of the land. When nothing more revealed itself to me, I gingerly stood. I had been hoping for a vantage point, as had existed in Malphas' territory, a ledge where I could see where I was meant to go. Instead, all I had was the strangely red grass and my human fear, an instinct telling me: *do not touch*.

I think it was out of instinct that I went down onto my knees as if in prayer. It was something I knew how to do and something that inspired in me a kind of certainty, the sense that I was doing something productive. I prayed for direction, a way to fulfil my purpose, which I held proudly in my heart.

Let me go to Asmodeus, my Prince of Lust, I begged, either to Asmodeus itself or some mighty power in Hell, or perhaps I was appealing to my own instincts to comprehend what I was supposed to do next. I needed a Knight of Hell, a rank I knew very little about.

When I opened my eyes, a path of pure black soil had emerged in the sea of grass. Inevitably, I thought of Moses as I stood and stepped into the bare soil, my feet gliding through upturned roots and loose dirt. I was careful not to touch the swaying edges of the grass, for I did not know what would become of me if I did.

My mind's eyes showed me all sorts of things: flesh that bubbled and bled off the bone. Death eternal, reliving the same agonising seconds over and over for however long I kept contact with the grass. A strange overtaking of my body, a force transforming it into a vessel, where the seeds of evil took root in my lungs and, bit by bit, destroyed the markers of my humanity, eating everything familiar away until I was a nameless demon myself.

Whether these thoughts were real or simply my fears, I did not test the theory. I knew already, based on Malphas' assertion that I had eaten from the realm and would be more 'settled', that maintaining my humanity might have been a battle I could not win. Over time, I guessed, my mortal form would change. How could it not? I had no concept of time here, but undoubtedly, even a second in Hell would alter my body.

The thought unnerved me. I wanted to be as I remembered; I wanted to hold onto the old Alessandro as long as I could. In truth, I wanted to retain the identity I'd had most of my life. To be the priest corrupted by the demon—not a disgraced, ex-communicated layman turned demonic. What did that say about me? Perhaps I romanticised my old station. Or perhaps I wanted God to see me; I wanted to fear God as much as I wanted Him to know I was blaspheming against him.

I did not want to lose the thing that made my actions sacrilegious. I wanted this to be a sin.

I bit down on my tongue to ground my wandering mind. No matter the why—I knew what I had to do. With Asmodeus and all the demons I would have to pleasure to reach my new God spurring me on, I walked that dry path with my traitorous mind evoking Exodus; it echoed in my skull, again and again:

"*. . .and the Lord drove the sea back by a strong east wind all night and made the sea dry land, and the waters were divided.*"

This is how I came to the library.

❧ 7 ❧

CHAPTER SEVEN

I do not know if it was an actual place or something Hell itself conjured for me, but it sprang up from the ground the way the church had where the lesser demons had impaled me. The dry path stopped abruptly, and the red grass shivered and danced in an unnatural wind I could not feel. Then, emerging chthonic, a white dusty stone rumbled out of the earth. Layered stone slabs as tall as myself began to rise, packed upon one another in the way of towering cathedrals, and within several of my panicked breaths, the structure rose to great heights. It was a spiralling monstrosity of nonsensical architecture.

I craned back, trying to see the top of it, shielding my face from the sudden storm of rock dust that was dredged up by the movement. When it finally subsided, an open archway appeared in front of me.

If ever there was such a definitive answer to a prayer for guidance, this was it.

I walked inside without fear.

It was not a structure that could have ever existed on earth. I could describe it as a set of ruined cathedrals stacked precariously upon one another, a building that required no natural laws to be in place. Gravity did not affect it, and nor did it seem structurally unsound, though there existed very little in the way of supporting beams. The arched doorway led into the lower level, a foyer-like expanse with cracked black and white tiles flecked with green. Scattered wooden desks lay about, suffering through various states of decay. It was only when I looked up and became confronted by the strange mishmash of levels, floating bookshelves, suspended rocky platforms and the like that I understood it to be a library.

Though, of course, like none I had ever encountered before.

The foyer had a staircase, one of those incredibly gaudy styles that split needlessly, both sets of stairs reaching the same landing. I climbed one side incautiously, drawn forward by an unnameable feeling. A familiar scent wafted to me. Books, aged leather, amber, the mildewed rot of tomes long left unattended. There was no sound save for the wind outside.

Level upon level of information spanned like this. Briefly, I was overcome by the sheer size of the place, and I could not comprehend what I was to learn in this collection of knowledge. I picked up the first book I came to, its red cover so worn the title had bled into the fabric, and when I opened it, I was confounded. I tried the next and the next, and only a few books had any sentences I could read fully.

Philosophy, astronomy, rhetoric, logic—there were sections dictated by signs in perfect Italian, but the books were hostage to an infernal language I could not comprehend. In fact, when I read, I felt the letters running from me, and if I was ever on the verge of understanding the words, they would shift and change to escape my comprehension.

I put down the tomes. I was only here for one thing—I

had asked to understand the next rank I was to encounter on my journey to Asmodeus. So, as ever before, I kept that impetus in my mind's eye and let my body settle until I felt the pull of direction.

I climbed. It was no easy task. The stairs that existed in the foyer did not exist on other levels, or at least in no helpful way. Some stairs floated aimlessly and led to nowhere. Others were upside down or placed along bookshelves, or shrunken as if for ants to use. It meant that, as my body felt called deeper and deeper into the chaotic structure, I was clambering up bookshelves and leaping to new platforms, and I was not by any stretch of the imagination a wildly athletic man. Coupled with my nudeness, I felt ashamed of how desperately I moved. But this was what I wanted, what I had committed to, and shame was God's domain.

The structure somehow settled in the upper reaches. Clouds surrounded me, and I could no longer see the bottom, which had been swallowed up by a thick nacreous, fog. The ceiling of this place was vaulted and supported by multiple cross-beams, so it resembled a barn, though the roof and walls were made of the same white stone as the rest of the place. The floors appeared to be a deep mahogany and the bookshelves were scarce. Most of them were pressed against the walls, leaving the centre of the room exposed. It was there I saw a sigil, very similar to that in Malphas' territory:

Cautiously, I walked to it. A plain-handled knife had been left in its centre. The blade appeared clean, and the sigil was dry of blood.

My understanding of seals and sigils was exceptionally limited, given their occult nature and the church's fear of such teachings. I knew vaguely of the Lesser Key of Solomon but had always been too frightened to read it. Holy men who had encountered demons or were scholars of demonology often had their expertise called upon, but I was too lowly a don to ever encounter them. Seals, as I understood them, should have warded demons off. But my blood had mingled with Malphas' and called it forth—a summoning, a covenant, a deal with a devil.

I stepped away from this seal. Was I in the Knight's territory, standing in amongst all this knowledge? When I had thought I wanted to know it, had I been led directly to it instead?

I turned and let myself move to the bookshelves, dragging my hands over the tomes until my fingers paused. It wasn't a natural decision. My whole body ceased moving over one particular tome. I pulled the book free, a thick thing inscribed with Latin, *De Daemonibus In Circulo Asmodei*.

On the demons in Asmodeus' circle.

I tried to open it from the first page, but the tome refused. It was as if all the pages were a singular piece, a thick wad. I tried the back cover and was met with the same resistance. But when I pressed upon the middle, the tome split open like ripe fruit. Unseen air flicked through the pages and settled upon a spread.

I read:

Furcas, eques inferni, cujus statio ei singularis est, qui viginti legiones daemonum sub eius imperio habet.

Furcas, the Knight of Hell, whose station is unique to him, who has twenty legions of demons under his command.

Nothing else appeared on the page. I had no compulsion to read further, and the knowledge settled in me that this Furcas was who I was after. Indeed, whose seal it must have been, spread on the wooden floor before me.

I went to it. I lowered my body before the sigil in supplication. I held the demon's name and title in my mind and rolled it over and over on my tongue. Furcas, the Knight of Hell. Furcas, I summon thee.

I reached into the circle, picked up the small knife, and dragged it across the palm of my hand, where I had made the same cut for Asmodeus—the scar remaining as the only blemish on my body—and for Malphas, though with much firmer pressure. Warm blood trickled like syrup down my palm, and the instant the first drop hit the waiting grooves, some force of magic seemed to pull it out of me. My blood fell quickly, almost eagerly, like the seal craved it. My vision blurred, and a haze of dizziness descended. Woozy, I lay down, waiting for the summons to be done.

I awoke to the clopping of hooves. Wearily, I blinked my eyes open. I could see nothing but the legs of the horse upon which the demon sat. Sandy-white, pale as the stone that surrounded us, the horse's colour reminded me of bone. Indeed, it seemed at odd places that osseous growths protruded from the flank, reminding me of sprouting fungi. I scanned for the feet of this newcomer, who undoubtedly was the Knight, if the horse was an indicator of this demon's rank. But there were no human feet in the stirrups, and, indeed, no stirrups nor saddle at all.

My voice caught in my throat. It was not quite a scream, but not an easy, happy sound either. Delayed in my understanding, the full sight of Furcas terrified me. I sat up in a rush, choking on my quick intake of breath. My palm, stained as it was with blood, slipped back as I scrambled away from the bloody seal. I almost prayed. I almost invoked God.

The muscular legs of the horse gave way to human flesh. Indeed, the flank of a human man seemed to split forth from between the horse's hair and then rise up into a man's torso—equally as pale as the horse's flank.

Furcas, Knight of Hell, took the form of a beautiful but intimidating centaur. Its human half was strong, big-bellied, with a long white beard that covered its navel. Muscle bulged in its arms and around its shoulders, and its unkempt beard and long white hair masked much of its face. Its eyes were a dazzling icy blue, and clutched in its clawed hand—fingers long and nails longer—was a spear.

Words failed me. I stared. I think this was the one that shocked me the most, out of all the forms of demons I had seen thus far. Every other form had been unknowable before the moment of my seeing them. But this? Centaurs were a myth to me, something confirmed as an impossibility—and here I was before one, staring at the sutured flesh between human skin and horse flank. The uncanniness of the human part of Furcas, with its all-seeing eyes and hollow cheekbones, only made its lower half more confronting. Its tail was like that of a human skeleton, without any flesh about it at all. It was forked at the end, and it whipped through the air like a cat's. I could do nothing except drop into a low bow, and with my forehead pressed to the ground, I hoped that would be enough to avoid any wrath.

I squeezed my eyes shut. With only the sound of its hooves clopping and my heavy breathing, I could vaguely tell it was circling me. Hesitantly, I craned to look at it. Furcas was not looking at me. It glanced around, seemingly confused, its eyes darting down to the seal where my blood stained the grooves. Furcas cocked its head and bore its sharp, shark-like teeth.

"Lord," I croaked out. Its eyes shot down to me then.

"The summonings I am used to drag me up to Earth," it said. Its voice was unlike anything I had ever heard. It felt ephemeral, somehow abstract, and not wholly physical. I could describe it like a whisper in the wind, a shadow out of the corner of my eyes. It spoke, and I could not be sure that it had. The end of its sentences felt to me like distant memories. "Rarely do I have requests to teach students already condemned to Hell."

Near delirious with confusion, feeling somehow like it had finished its sentence hours ago, I dragged myself upright, hoping this more grounded position would help me focus. "I have not been condemned." Surprisingly, my voice came out harsh. Defiant. "I have entered Hell of my own volition."

Furcas' eyes slid towards me, expression dazzled like it was seeing me for the first time. Its horse body moved around me, eyes never straying as it took me in.

"I see a naked, decrepit human man. Plagued by lust, apparently, if you have fallen into Asmodeus' domain. But, if you have wandered this far into Hell without any of my infernal brethren stopping you, that suggests a mark of wit. A savvy nature. Do you know who I am?"

I recall being frightened to admit how little I knew. From the way it circled me and its talk of summonings, I gathered it assumed I had summoned it for—well, because I wanted

Furcas and not as a means to some salacious end. I opened my mouth and regurgitated the titles and honorifics the text had bestowed upon Furcas, the Knight of Hell.

It narrowed its eyes at me, and I knew that *it* knew I wasn't truly here for it. In a desperate scrabble, I looked about, pointing at the rows of books. "Is this your library?"

Though its expression remained cloudy, Furcas nodded. "Rhetoric, logic, astronomy. . .I teach it all. All the knowledge I craved in Heaven that was denied to me was given to me here. Is this what you wish to learn?"

I hesitated. My eyes dragged over its body and lower to the cock between its equine legs. I shuddered, unclear if I was feeling revulsion or attraction, or that strange mix of both, if taboo was lighting a fire in me, if I could imagine that thing sliding into me, gaping me, splitting me apart.

My cheeks were burning up. I bit my tongue and looked away.

"Tell me why you are here, little human," it said with preternatural calm. "Before you anger me."

I believed wholeheartedly that Furcas' rage would be destructive. It frightened me more than Malphas had; this pared-back desert of a building, these empty halls echoing with lost tomes and dust and silence—a demon whose knighthood was exclusive, who chose to live seemingly isolated.

So, I told it everything in lurid detail, sparing nothing. I invoked Asmodeus as if calling upon my great Lord might spare me from any harm.

When I was finished, Furcas leaned forward. Its curiosity wafted off it, and a grin pricked at its lips.

"You," it said, disbelief clouding its eyes, "summoned *Asmodeus?*"

I didn't understand its tone. Was it astonished at my bravery? Was it disbelieving that I had managed it?

I opened my mouth to clarify, and it leaned down, human

fingers ghosting over my lips. The claws, which were over-grown yellowed nails sharpened to a point, stung as they pressed into the tender flesh of my face. It peeled my lower lip away from my teeth, then dragged those claws across my cheek firmly enough to leave a mark.

"A priest turned expert summoner," Furcas murmured. "Asmodeus is not any easy force to pull from the dredges of Hell. Do you understand? Either you are lying to me, or you intrinsically possess the skill plenty of your mortal brethren try to perfect over decades of study, failed summonings, an, on occasion, covenants made. They make deals with lesser demons before they can summon someone stronger. They gain a little knowledge in exchange for their soul. A gift for a gift." It assessed me, eyes raking down. "But perhaps the well of your lust was so deep even Asmodeus could not deny you."

I did not want to jump up and exclaim, "*Yes, precisely!*" when it seemed to me that Furcas was implying my soul to be so dripping with lust and longing it had had enough power to call forth Asmodeus. Thinking back on it, I did not recall that first summoning to be difficult. I had longed for a master of sexual depravity to have me. Asmodeus had answered. Was that because I was powerful? Or because Asmodeus had taken pity on me?

With a bravery I had so rarely possessed, I stood at my full height. My head barely came up to Furcas' chest. I could have walked forward and had its pinkish nipple between my teeth, its long white beard a pillow upon which I might rest.

Again, like many of the demons I had encountered, its attractiveness was not native to it—unlike Asmodeus, whose human-like body had incited a fever in me, Furcas terrified me more than aroused me. Yet, locked in that complex string of emotions, I saw myself doing things that might have once disgusted me. I could see my mouth encir-cling the oversized equine cock, engorging myself on it, turning my body and slipping back onto it, ruining my insides, feeling it in my guts—Furcas' hand slipped beneath my chin.

"You wish to survive this place in order to reach our Lord Asmodeus, King of this Circle, Prince of Lust?"

I nodded pensively into the support of its palm. Furcas pressed its pink tongue to its teeth; the flesh bulged between the filed canines, spilled out between them like minced meat.

"I can impart my wisdom onto you, little priest," it whispered. "For a price, of course."

I'm ashamed to say my eyes wandered, dipping down to that place where, on a human man, a cock would sit. My eyes moved to gaze over a horse-like flank. But Furcas saw me staring. It chuckled low in its throat.

"I am sure that is the price you would like to pay," it said and then seemed to stop itself from finishing the thought. Its fingers drifted from my chin, and I swayed without the additional support.

"The price. . .?" I murmured, hoping to clarify.

But it curled its lip and hissed something too softly for me to hear. Those strange eyes darted to me. "Later. Let me impart my knowledge upon you first."

I did not fight it. It moved away from the circle and sat cat-like on its haunches. Its tail—serpentine, bare-boned and forked at the end—rested gracefully across its hooves. I pointedly did not look at what I knew to be between its legs and sat in a way I would not be tempted to see it, for I feared to anger Furcas.

Like this, we began to talk. Furcas taught, and I listened and learned. Hours passed, and perhaps days, too, sat before it in the abandoned library. It seemed to take pleasure in teaching, and since I was there to give pleasure, I couldn't deny it. When my attention wandered, its human mouth hissed at me and demanded my attention return. Quickly, I gathered all my focus, and gave it to this centaur demon before me.

At first, Furcas taught me more about the hierarchy of Hell—that it had been given the distinctive title of Knight for its chivalry and loyalty during the Fall. When I asked to whom it had been most loyal, it clicked its tongue at me.

"Questions are an inevitable consequence of my tutelage, but I do not always have to answer."

Which was the politest way a demon could have told me to shut up. It had an honour about it, or a belief in itself and its goodness, as if being confined and condemned to the hellish pits hadn't undermined its honour. I came to understand that it did not revel in wrongdoing nor encourage such a thing in the way many of its brethren did. It had taken a deal of sorts, chased knowledge, and refused to give up that pursuit. It had been a servant, no archangel nor favourite of the Lord on high. All it had done was refuse to serve humanity without earning something in return.

"You believed you were above humans?" I clarified.

It said immediately, without emotion, "I am above humans. Anything that fell from Heaven is."

In truth, this did not frighten me. I understand God had made us in the image of his Son, and then declared us above the angels. I had been taught Lucifer's defiance of this had sparked a war. That pride had corrupted Lucifer Morningstar, the adversary, Satan, who had exclaimed:

> *'I will ascend to Heaven;*
> *above the stars of God*
> *I will set my throne on high;*
> *I will sit on the mount of assembly*
> *in the far reaches of the north,*
> *I will ascend above the heights of the clouds;*
> *I will make myself like the Most High.'*

"Our great Lord Satan had been made perfect," Furcas clarified for me. "The greatest beauty, the most perfect angel, formed just so. Imagine a thousand years passing where you are one thing, only for your father to take it all away. To bestow status instead on undeserving mortal life. God's decision enraged my Lord. It enraged a third of God's angels. When I learned that I, too, would need to bow before humanity, who might summon me to answer their questions of rhetoric, logic, or astronomy and provide me nothing in return, is it any wonder I chose to fall and carve out a new life here?"

I did not answer. Something about considering Lucifer, who had been my greatest adversary for most of my life, frightened me. I'd been an agent of God, and thinking of *Satan*, let alone speaking of him so candidly, had always seemed akin to invoking him or begging him to turn his eye upon you. To think of him like this—a being scorned, a role reversed, an identity confused—made me near empathetic. I baulked at that realisation. My heart began to race. I was sure Furcas noticed, for it stopped talking and leaned forward.

I did not open my eyes. I tried to find comfort in that dark nothingness, hoping I could regain my composure even as nausea twisted in my stomach. Clawed fingers pressed into my soft palate, and only when it began to sting did I blink my eyes open.

Furcas had grown exceptionally close. Its nostrils flared, and the white whiskers of its beard tickled my cheek. It was inhaling me. My body shivered, like some essence was being willed out of my flesh through the pores. Furcas sucked its teeth.

"Frightened, are you?"

I might have laughed if my body could have moved. But I

was locked in a trance before it, too nervous to shift away lest those claws slice my throat. Sweat I hadn't noticed began to drip into my eyes, and very gently, Furcas leaned forward and licked my brow clean.

"What have my brethren done about you?" it asked me, pressing for more details. "You mentioned lesser demons and Malphas—who did not enter you?"

It turned my chin this way and that. It did not bother with pretence, not hiding its assessment of me as its eyes raked over my face and body. I opened my mouth to reply, and it squeezed my cheeks together so hard my lips pursed and my face practically distended.

"How did you enter here, little priest?" it whispered, and only when my eyes widened did it release the pressure on my face.

"W-what?" I gasped and then coughed, sliding back ever so slightly on the wooden floor to put even an inch of distance between the two of us. Furcas allowed this with only a raise of its arched brow to suggest it knew I was frightened.

"I believe you heard me clearly."

"Yes," I said, "Yes, I heard you."

Frustration gleamed in the demon's eyes. "How did you come to be in Hell as you are?"

Stop talking back. Who do you think you are?

Blushing, I explained, "I—my Prince told me to find it. To walk into Hell. I tricked a bishop and had him lead me to the Cave of the Sibyl, and there I performed a ritual. The gates opened. But I also. . .I stabbed myself."

I didn't say the rest, but Furcas, with its great knowledge of rhetoric and logic, could hear the unspoken words. It tipped its head thoughtfully. "Ah. . .you can't tell if you're dead or alive?"

I thought of the numerous notes on my scent the demons had given me. That I reeked of the light and of life, like godliness and incense and oxygen had knitted into my skin. I thought of the hags in Malphas' territory who had fed me to settle my stomach and keep me grounded in this realm.

I told Furcas, "I think I am alive."

It nodded thoughtfully, standing and walking to the bookshelves. "I believe you are. Some humans have entered Hell before, you know. *Entered* being the crucial term there. Plenty of humanity's souls have haunted the abyss for a long while. But, of the way you entered, you are not the first."

My stomach twisted, and heat fired behind my eyes. My heart raced, and I realised I did not know what I was feeling —except terrible, and worthless, and barely alive. "Who?" I demanded. "For Asmodeus?"

Furcas looked at me over the shelves. The milky white eyes unsettled me from this distance, blurring as they did into the demon's beard and hair. It bore those sharp teeth at me and began to cackle. The laughter went on, distended and elongated and entirely unnecessary. I baulked standing before Furcas, whose old face bobbed oddly as if decapitated, body hidden as it was behind the shelves. Then, Furcas' jaw cracked and inexplicably began to lower. It dropped uncomfortably wide and then wider still; I saw the yawning chasm of its tar-black throat, the slate grey of its tongue like meat about to turn. The sharp teeth were rotten in places, and the gums were green. The jaw lowered and lowered until the impossibility of the mouth was near hilarious—though I could not laugh. I could not even dream of laughing. Pink fleshy tendon knitted the top and bottom rows of teeth together, and as the jaw stretched, so too did this poor suture, which at times began to snap.

I became so dizzy with fear that I began to scream.

❧ 8 ❧

CHAPTER EIGHT

"**W**hat do you want?" I howled, not understanding the change in Furcas or this demonic energy. "*What do you want from me?*"

With terrifying speed, it rounded the corner and galloped at me. A board cracked beneath the sudden force of its approach, and I screamed and went to my knees. Furcas stopped before it crushed me and ran its fingers through my hair, gripping hard.

"Stop screaming," it hissed, and I clamped my mouth shut. Tears fell—I could not stop them leaking from my eyes.

"You are a stupid fool of a human," Furcas told me. "About as pathetic as your kind can get. But you have also a misplaced wisdom or a luck—something favours you. You could not have made it this far otherwise. I will tell you this. Your jealousy of other humans, whether they have entered Hell for Lord Asmodeus or not, will be your undoing. The Prince might find it sweet for the first blink of an eye, but it has had a millennium of whores, demonic or human, or the occasional angelic on the verge of losing its status. Surely you know you are not special?"

"I know that," I said. I had already come to this conclusion. "But I am human. I feel certain ways, and sometimes I can't always help it."

"You have let yourself be fucked and used by plenty of demons. Do you fear Asmodeus will fuck other holes in its wait for you to reach it?"

Furcas loosened its tight grip on my hair as it spoke. I slumped. Its question defeated me.

I struggled to form the words. To explain to this demon the complexities of human desire, of my insecurity, of the greatest sacrifice I had made. Everything I was had been reduced to this, naked and shivering before a demonic centaur. Could something as ancient as Furcas or, indeed, my Lord Asmodeus, ever understand the act of devoting one's life if one was *immortal*?

"Tell me," it whispered. "Speak to me your fears."

Shaking, I let it all out. "I am jealous, sometimes. Often fearful. I have no worth except for my body and my devotion, but I will give it to Lord Asmodeus, as I promised it on Earth. And I have given the entirety of myself. Even my mortal life." I looked up at Furcas, who stared down at me, hooves clopping as it shifted its weight. "So I am not jealous of Asmodeus using other creatures. I am scared that, by the time I reach it, it won't remember me. That I'll be forgettable. That it'll... it'll all have been for nothing."

The last words turned to a whisper, strangled high.

"Then you must stand out, don't you think? You must show Asmodeus just how willing you are to become its toy. Even to the extent of pleasuring me, an old man with the body of a horse. For this repulses you. I can see it in your eyes. You may wonder about the size of my cock pressing into you and bulging out your stomach, but you wish it was attached to something you could find pretty in the right lighting." Furcas' touch became soft. I couldn't quite comprehend the shift in its attitude; the wisdom turned to wild and unfettered insanity, curtailed once more to encourage me to bend over for it.

I would have done it anyway. Did it not know that? I needed no convincing on my journey to Asmodeus.

But perhaps it *is the one who needs convincing.*

Yes, that was it, wasn't it? A wise and learned creature whose pride had brought it to the depths of Hell in pursuit of knowledge. . . that kind of creature could not happily enter a human. But in service to its Lord, and perhaps as a means of having me owe something, it could do it. Perhaps even with joy.

"You would do that for me?" I clarified, making it obvious I understood Furcas was framing this as a kindness. It nodded slowly, long-nailed fingers stroking through my hair. I let it drag those fingers down and catch on my lip and let them slip ever so slightly into my mouth, where I tasted the dust of old tomes still coating the tips of its fingers. As it glided those fingers out, I said, "For what price?"

Its eyes flashed at me, and a low chuckle rumbled in its chest. "Ahh. . .how smart of you to ask, little lamb."

It assessed me, and I waited. What would it want? For it to have been dismissed by the angelic creatures in Heaven, for it to turn its back and gladly walk to Hell, what could I offer it to make my hole worth its while? I envisioned it asking me to petition for it, taking some plea all the way to Asmodeus. Would it ask for more books? More knowledge? A bigger library?

And what wouldn't you do, whorish priest? You have made it clear your body is forfeit in pursuit of Asmodeus. Becoming a pack mule is little strain on a body already crushed and reshaped by monstrous lengths.

I jolted.

The journey didn't matter. That I would become a

messenger did not matter. What disturbed my soul was that, after decades, I had never once been a messenger for God. Instead, in worship of a lesser demon, I would do its bidding.

Behold, I send my messenger before your face, who will prepare your way before you.

Furcas leaned down and bared its teeth at me. It was terrifying. Then it licked out, strange human tongue flattening against my cheek as if to savour the sweat pooling.

"Little Alessandro, with your body so perfectly lithe. . .your hips jutting from your skin like osseous handholds, your waist small enough for my hands to wrap around you wholly. . .I understand why my Lord Asmodeus is testing you. I could ask you for knowledge, or I could ask you to beg our Lord for a moment of its time. But you have fallen into my lap and listened so well to my conversations that you do not disgust me nearly as much as you first did. The sound of your voice excites me. I can feel it, the way it pitches high when you're frightened. And so I have been imagining it. All the sounds you might make, the way you will writhe when my overbearing weight holds you down. How you will arch your back and shudder as I enter you. How you might sound when I use you without mercy—for there is no better way to test your devotion to Asmodeus than to withstand my attempt to break you."

My breathing grew rapid. Transfixed, locked halfway between lust and fear, I could do nothing but watch the demon; too frightened was I to move or look away. Furcas stroked my cheek and smiled. "All I want from you in exchange," it kissed my forehead, "is to hear you *scream*."

My voice lodged in my throat. A shiver passed over my body, and I involuntarily convulsed. All my bodily systems turned riotous, for both desire and fear fought to take control, and in the ensuing struggle, I found myself incapable of moving.

Furcas' hand moved up the side of my cheek to the top of my head. Roughly, it forced me onto the ground. Crowded in on either side by its four legs, with my head pressed up to the underside of its belly, I felt at once claustrophobic and strangely at peace. From this vantage, I could see its cock— long, flared—twitching to life.

"Help it along," Furcas said, voice low and airy.

I shivered. I had never seen one so large or lightly coloured. Hesitantly, I crawled forward to be close to it. It smelled of sweat and something sweetly acrid, a scent enhanced by the translucent fluid pooling at the head.

I went to the underside of it, kissing the place when the length joined the balls, which were warm against the palms of my hands. Moving my fingers gently, I cupped and moved them, felt the weight of them, the heft. I opened my lips and put one in my mouth, hand fondling the other before I passed my mouth over that as well. They were softer than expected. Gravity helped me; they sank onto my tongue with ease. The taste was murky, layered with sweat, salt, the dank of unwashed skin—an appetiser in anticipation of the main course. I dragged my tongue up the underside of the long cock and found myself near frightened when I reached the head and found the flared top and puckered hole already furiously leaking. Furcas stomped somewhat impatiently, but what made this unique from other times I had been forced on my knees—save, of course, the type of cock I planned to service—was that Furcas' human arms could not easily reach me.

So every movement I was to make or not make, every lick and kiss and full-throated suck I would offer came down to me. I would not be forced; I would have to prove my desire.

Resist the devil, and he will flee from you.

By the same logic: embrace the devil, and he will come to you.

I embraced Furcas with my mouth. I opened and tried to wrap my lips around the pulsing cock. I peeled my teeth away as far as I could, afraid to nick the most sensitive skin, afraid to pollute its pleasure and therefore its opinion of me.

Furcas made a grunting noise that nearly warped into a whinny, and my stomach twisted, and my heart sped at the wrongness of this.

Demons are fine, Malphas with its raven-head would have been fine, but when one's lower half is horse-like, where do you draw the line? Clearly, I had not drawn the line. I was on my knees, rutting up into my palm with my cock as hard as ever, sucking desperately on what little of the equine member I could fit into my mouth.

Then, roughly, Furcas stepped away from me. The hooves clopped back, and I craned my neck as its face came into view. The demon was looking down at me, eyes alive with interest but otherwise wearing an expression I could not read. Without another word, it raised one of its horse legs and jabbed it into my side. I flinched away, understanding belatedly it wanted me to roll onto my stomach, and the instant I did it was upon me, cock rubbing over the cleft of my ass.

Instinctively, in anticipation, I whimpered.

The size was not something I had encountered before—or rather, the *length*. Of all the demons I had encountered, Asmodeus' cock had been the one to fit perfectly, stretching and filling and reaching in all directions the most perfect amount. The two demons that had pulled me onto the crucifix had been large and similarly as huge as Furcas. But neither of them had been this long nor this dangerously shaped.

Indeed, it *did* feel dangerous, then. I felt certain something vital in me would tear or bleed. But I thought also of what I had promised to Asmodeus, and to myself, of the kind of person I had vowed I would become. Scripture inevitably came to me, then. Do you know, I felt that I could use most of my passages in my prayers, and they still held true when I meant them for Asmodeus. And so Jonah 2:9 filled my mind:

"But I with the voice of thanksgiving will sacrifice to you; what I have vowed I will pay. Salvation belongs to the Lord!"

Salvation belonged to Asmodeus. I would offer every part of myself to these demons as an instrument, a means to achieving that salvation. The fear stopped. Pain in this place was only temporary; my body was no longer human. I could be pushed to the uttermost limit and not die.

"Open for me," Furcas growled, and I reached back with both hands to spread my cheeks to it. My face dug into the hard ground, and something in my spine popped from this angle. I imagined the depth of it, how it might press so far inside it would push my bulging stomach to the ground.

Without any preparation, Furcas tried to push inside.

I sighed with wanton anticipation. The pressure of the head against me felt not quite right. Part of me longed to give, for my hole to shudder open and take the impossibly sized length and bear the pain of it. But the reality was simple: without preparation, I could not open for it. Thus, Furcas had me change positions. It lowered itself so my mouth could suck at its cock again, and it could use its human hands to relax me and pleasure me. It knelt down for my ease and—my heart shivered. Was this affection? Was this a kindness? My experience with human sexuality was non-existent, but I had imagined, somewhere beneath the lust and the depravity, for something. . .something like this. . .

I want to hear you scream.

I came back to myself, for this was not a kindness. This was not for my benefit, but for Asmodeus', Furcas' Lord, and Furcas itself might take me to the brink, leave me gaping and weak, but it would not be allowed to impale me to death.

It slipped a finger in and pumped it in and out of me with no slowness or kindness. I groaned. Pleasure had me instantly relaxed, and I spread my legs, a sight that made Furcas chuckle. My eagerness was palpable. Even from that single finger, I felt wanton and wild.

It waited very little time to slip another finger in, then another, and another, until four fingers were moving slowly in and out, and Furcas was murmuring to me, fingers from its other hands gently stoking my cock. I kept bucking up towards the touch, for the slightest friction drove me insane, but Furcas kept hushing me, waving its hand inside my hole until it forced its thumb inside, too, and I cried out.

Its knuckles slid deep into me, hand elongated and fingers reaching for my insides before it curled into a fist. It spat onto its hand, and the slickness made it easier for Furcas to move. The only sounds were our heavy panting, my cries of pleasure and often pain, and then the wet *shlick* of its fist filling me.

Minutes went by with me arched like that, eyes rolling to the back of my skull. Furcas stared down at me, chilly eyes boring into my soul, and then it came to some decision. It punched down into my hole with such force a scream was ripped out of me.

I cried out, tears springing into my eyes, and every forceful thrust forward had my eyes rolling back, had me crying, had me limply jerking from the ache, the sharp stretch, and the pleasure pulsing out from my prostate.

"God's puppet," Furcas said in wonderment, "and now mine."

It pulled its fist free and rolled me, not gently. I flopped onto my stomach, moaning weakly. Cold air pricked at my entrance, and I could feel the hole pulsing weakly, squeezing around nothing. Furcas made a low moan of approval.

It guided me to slide between its equine legs, straddling

me, and pressed again to my backside, clear slick fluid oozing onto my back as dragged its cock wetly over my ass.

"For my Lord," Furcas said. "As repayment for this bastion Asmodeus let me build here, for its honouring of the promise made on the precipice of the Fall, I will breach this human and fill him with seed and a thirst for knowledge: to know the True Form of our shared Lord and to satisfy it for eternity."

It mounted me completely and pushed the flared head of its cock to my open, pulsing hole. Clear fluid spouted from the tip, so much so I could feel it running over the cleft of my ass and down into the gap, down my inner thighs. My own cock was desperate for friction, but from this angle, I couldn't do anything but let Furcas have its way. And it did have its way.

The demon-centaur reared up with an excited whinny and breached my body.

My head fell limply to the floor. There was a long moment of incomprehension where I could feel the bulge as it shuddered into my stomach, and I became like a pocket in which Furcas' cock could sit. My hole pulsed rapidly around Furcas, and I realised I was groaning and crying out, my body spasming for the sheer overwhelm of the sensation. The pain came next, as the initial shock ebbed out of my body. But I kept trembling.

"*You're so. . . big!*" I cried out, and Furcas laughed.

"Little human, I have barely entered you."

I frowned. Furcas was not moving, allowing me to relax, and I pressed my hand to my stomach, certain I had felt it bulging just moments ago. As I relaxed, though, I understood only the great flared head of the cock had pushed inside.

Fuck. Oh, fuck.

I—how could I *do* this?

Furcas' massive hands stroked my torso, so big they could

easily interlock at my front. They encompassed the entire waist.

"I think you are ready now."

I strained. I felt its cock quiver into me and then hammer down.

I howled. Bright, shocking pain blazed into my body. Straining, almost fearfully, my body lurched away, but Furcas put a hoofed foot against my back and pressed. It felt so large that I could barely squirm against it, and my body collapsed to the ground, ass raised but otherwise still. Like that on the ground, crying out, I choked on a plea. I broke a little, then. I cried. I begged: *"Please, please, please."*

Furcas either did not hear or did not care. It did not stop fucking me. And when I opened my mouth, nothing came out except my desperate moans.

Pathetic.

With a slowness, Furcas pressed down on my back and pushed inside to bottom out. I strained around, trying to see how much of it my body could accommodate. Little more than a third of its length had pressed into me when my body began to convulse.

Looking back now, I believe it was shock. A body pushed to its limits too quickly, a mind equally whorish and terrified, too frightened and too aroused to demand the demon stop. Because despite the fear and the pain and the instinct in my body to get away, I lay there moaning, reaching back to spread my cheeks to further ease the access to my hole.

I wanted it. I *wanted* it.

Still, I trembled with shock as it pressed and prodded, trying to loosen the tightness. My eyes rolled back into my skull, and saliva leaked from my mouth. Every moment dragged on an eternity, every moment of pain carrying with it the outline of pleasure. Impaled like that on cock, I grew so weak and full of feeling that my arms dropped limply to my side, where they dragged against the wooden boards. Furcas used me. It used me over and over like that, ramming into me, its massive cock levering my body open as it ignored my uselessly limp top half that was battling to remain conscious. I came a number of times just like that, my cock untouched, prostate pulsing, until I felt spent and slipped out of my reality to the edge of unconsciousness.

What was happening to my body seemed to be just on the right side of the outright impossible. I had no understanding of what magic was at play here; perhaps Furcas was perforating my insides as it went, and I was healing over and over. But as my body adjusted and my hole loosened, I reached a new state of being. My entire body was a hole for it to use, and I became distantly comfortable with my new reality.

If that was all I was, if *this* was how I could worship, then I was glad for it.

As my body gave, Furcas recognised the relaxation. It grunted, satisfied, and said, "That's it. Open for me. Open for me, whore." It pounded down into me, and I cried out, unabashed, gleeful. "Take it. Let yourself be reshaped to my member. Let your body change; you are nothing but a toy."

"*Yes,*" I cried out desperately, and as I opened my mouth, my words devolved into pleasured babbling, moans truncated by sharp intakes of breath and the beat of the demon's cock slamming into me.

When it finally came, hot warmth spurted into my body. I shivered and moaned, my pleasure intensifying as I heard Furcas make sounds of satisfaction. I craned around. It had its head up to the ceiling, both its human hands splayed on my back. My hole squeezed and pulsed around its cock, and it made a sensitive hiss as it slipped free, wet, spent length spilling excess seed onto the floorboards. I collapsed to the ground, panting hard. Cum leaked from me. I could feel it glugging free, and my own spent cock lay limp between my legs. But something was different.

Furcas moaned and reached for me. I felt it touching me —touching something that was not my hole. Or at least, not quite.

"You've slipped out," Furcas said.

My stomach plummeted. I reached back to where it was touching me. Something was. . . outside of me. The flesh there was soft and sensitive. I couldn't see it, but I could feel it from where it had spilled.

I had—prolapsed.

A great fear came over me. I made a noise of upset and tensed, expecting pain, though none came.

Furcas came closer, hooves stomping. I thought, distantly, it was reaching to pat me as if I were a pet, but instead it gripped a fistful of my hair and wrenched me upwards. I yelled and pressed weakly at its hands, then gave up and let my body hang limply.

"Such a slut," it said, shaking me. "Well done. I thought for sure you would break. But you pulled through even with your body like this."

I moaned a little at its words; praise-adjacent, *almost* a compliment. Furcas dropped me back down to the cum-soaked boards.

Exhaustion hit me. "I still have. . .so many more demons to service."

"Not just on your journey to Asmodeus," Furcas murmured. "For the rest of eternity. Used over and over— that is your destiny, now that you have turned from God."

The structure around us began to crumble. Bricks and stones neatly folded in on one another, undoing the mess of the ruined library I had climbed. Soon, there was only a rickety wooden platform upon which I stood. The outside, which had been that red field, consisted of nothingness. A stone cliff had appeared out of nowhere. I could make it if I leapt.

The floorboards, still etched with Furcas' sigil, glowed a pinkish red.

"Good luck, little priest," Furcas whispered. Its form was already disintegrating, its voice as distant as ever. "And should you ever crave to learn the dark arts, call upon me."

"Wait," I murmured. "You can't just—*please* don't leave me like this!"

I could have sworn that beneath those bushy brows, Furcas winked.

An instant later, and the demon was gone.

CHAPTER NINE

I lay there feeling sorry for myself for what felt like eons.

I had never—well, I'd never encountered this before and was unsure of the risks. I waited in vain for my body to heal itself, as all things had so far in Hell, but the canal remained as it was: turned inside out, pink and raw.

After an hour or so, the feeling changed. Concern no longer bothered me. In fact, the more I thought about it, the more my flaccid cock twitched to life.

I had been used so thoroughly, so completely, that my body had broken. A demolition of my insides, which spilled out of me. It aroused me, the knowledge that my body had been reduced to this. I put my hand between my legs and squeezed my cock, deciding slowly—perhaps not even consciously—to pleasure myself lying in the aftermath of Furcas' orgasm.

When I came, I expected the bliss to buckle to shame, as it often did. I expected pain to start up suddenly in my abdomen—but again, there was none.

Part of me thought I should try to stuff it back inside me, but another thought there were more blissful ways for that to happen. So it was that I stood like that, sweating and flushed and prolapsed, and made my way onwards.

I recounted my journey thus far. The lesser demons, the president, and the knight.

The next trial I was to face was an Earl of Hell.

I had only the hope it would be somewhat kind—a stupid and childish thought, given what I'd already encountered in Hell. But I set out stumbling, my body shivering with ecstasy.

I had to jump from the flimsy wooden structure and onto the cliff that had risen from nothingness. Slick black stone faced me with multiple jagged handholds, and a platform of rock jutted out towards me. Overhead from this platform, the cliff sloped downwards, but I caught a glimpse of what I assumed was a path.

That way, my heart said. I hesitated at the ledge, afraid of leaping and the way it might hurt my already sore body, but with nothing else to do, I embraced the possibility of my demise and leapt.

My feet met the other side with a grunt, half slipping on the wet rock. The air chilled my body, and I became acutely aware of my nether region, which still pulsed with that confused mix of excitement and discomfort. Ignoring it, I got to my feet and began to climb onto the new path.

The landscape changed immediately. Gone was the deadly red grass and trembling structure that had housed Furcas. In its place spanned a black ocean, traversable only by a tenuous rock bridge. I ignored the human fear at the height and the prospect of the fall and walked solemnly across the bridge. My destination was a blur. A wall of fog made it impossible to tell what lay in the distance, though I felt compelled to move forward regardless. Then, as I stepped into the mists, the temperature dropped. A brittle cold spiked through me. Clouds rolled in overhead, and the orange-red glow of Hell's eternal sunset turned a shade of grey. Thunder boomed. The sky lit up with sharp bursts of lightning. As the wind and a light rain began to pelt down upon me, I lowered myself to the ground and shivered in place. The thunder boomed closer. I slipped backwards, nearly toppling off the edge—and I heard laughter.

Move. You need to move.

This was simply another trial. *Trust in the Lord*— Asmodeus would not pit me against a trial it did not think I could overcome. I knew this in my heart of hearts, and I pulled myself back to my senses, standing braced for another gust of wind. Arm raised to shield my eyes, I moved as quickly as my body allowed, hobbling across the thin rock path and refusing to look down at the dark waves swirling beneath me. They crashed loudly against the base of this dangerous path, and even from this height, salt spray spritzed over my face. But it did not matter. I had to keep moving.

From the shadows, somewhere within the storm clouds, I heard that laughter again. It boomed like the thunder, deep and terrifying like a witch's cackle. With a maniacal edge to it, I imagined that's what it was: a witch, crazed, come to prevent my journey for whatever reason.

The fog had begun to clear, and I squinted through the storm, relieved to see that the thin stone bridge widened and spilled into a structure that looked suspiciously man-made: perfect stone, a platform surrounded by crags that sprouted from the mountain. Walled-in on either side, it gave the appearance of something safe. Faintly, I could see the ground shimmer as part of it dipped unevenly, but the platform rock appeared too perfectly smooth for this to be a natural divot.

That—was a sigil!

"*Who are you?*" I shouted at the next bark of laughter. And then, "*I must see an Earl of Hell!*"

"There are no Earls of Hell," it shouted. "No Earls who would see a human, either! There is nothing here for you! Nothing, nothing! "

A contradiction. I would have reasoned more, but the storm was growing—I ran full speed to the supposed safety of the platform, ignoring the danger of the wet rock and the discomfort in my lower body. Safety first. Adrenaline drowned out all other messages.

The cackling turned sour, almost fearful. The voice, which had been deep, raised several octaves. "Flee from this place! You are in danger!"

I ignored it.

Again, the voice came, "If you step there, you will die! You will die immediately!"

It sounded sincere. Its voice cracked, and it whined like a wounded animal. The voice went high and pained, the cry swallowed by the violent waves and the sound of the growing storm. I still could not see this thing, but I knew, as certainly as I knew my true nature, that this thing was deceiving me.

This one—most certainly a demon—I had not summoned, though as I grew closer to the platform, I confirmed that waiting for me was its sigil. Whether my blood would summon the Earl or bind this one to listen to me, I did not know. Was it an Earl? If so, why this charade?

In the end, it did not matter to me. Demons were deceivers. I had known that my whole life, and I still recalled it at that moment: humanity was not well-liked here, no matter if parts of me had use to them.

The path to the platform widened, and my stomach rushed up into my throat with sudden relief. Too soon—I heard the air hiss at my back and I turned in time to see a creature rushing me. I only caught a glimpse: a hart, with antlers long and shedding in red, ropey strings. It connected to a human-esque body covered in light brown fuzz, and an erect barbed cock poked towards me through the fur. At its back, two leathery wings sprouted, and a fiery tail whipped towards me, and the creature shrieked. Flame shot forward, and its eyes went wide with glee.

I slid away, rolling hard. Scrabbling up, I rushed to the sigil and threw myself to the knife, waiting poised on the ground. I slit the palm of my hand open and managed to slap it down onto the sigil just as two hands gripped at my ankles and wrenched me down.

I screamed and thrashed.

"You'll die here, stupid whore. You'll be ripped to shreds. I will throw your corpse to my armies and let them play with you until your body breaks apart; you will be fucked until you are a pile of bones crusted with the ejaculate of a thousand demons! I will *destroy you!* You should have never entered here!"

I tried to invoke Asmodeus—I said, "*Asmo—*"

"I have twenty-six legions of deprived demons ready for you. You cannot wander this land freely, human whore!"

"I belong to Asmodeus!" I howled.

I couldn't see its expression, but I felt the slackening of its grip. Half a second, maybe less; shock that registered in its body first. I did not wait. Viciously, I kicked out of its grasp and crawled back to the sigil. The cut on my hand was already stuffed with sand and dirt, clogged to the point it was not bleeding. The knife scraped the stone as I picked it up and ripped it across my forearm. The cut opened immediately. Blood spilled onto the sigil, and the demon behind me screamed with fury.

On my knees, I was at a standstill when I turned and saw it bolting towards me. *Move. Move!* But I didn't. I watched it rush me and did not even bring the knife up to my defence. Call it blood loss or a strange form of demonic worship, but I did not think once about my own wellbeing.

The demon's hoofed foot crossed the delineation of the sigil.

Everything went white.

🌸 10 🌸

CHAPTER TEN

My vision seemed to vanish. Hell turned impossibly bright, and I was blown out of the circle. Time must have passed, for when I finally pushed myself upright, the demon in the sigil was—different. Very different.

Standing before me was no demon at all but an angel.

I sat up and stared at it. My guard had gone up, as if seeing any reminder of the holy symbols or great angels I had abandoned sent my body into a panic. Grunting—for do remember, I was still at this point significantly *prolapsed*—I carefully crawled towards it.

"Why bother with the deception now?" I said. "I know your nature. You are no angel."

Indeed, the demon appeared like many of the church's depictions of the winged creatures. There was none of the terrifying, unknowable nature of the angels as spoken of in the Bible. This creature *glowed*. Alabaster skin so smooth, it evoked polished marble. Its hair was a light gold that curled over its chest and nipples, hiding what might have been budding breasts or a soft pectoral. Yes, I could not ascertain what I was looking at from first view; the creature before me was so perfectly ambiguous. It had a strongly angled face, delicate lips blushing near red as if a cherry had burst and stained them. Its eyes were hazel, and long lashes gave the impression of someone particularly demure. It held itself similarly. Beautiful, enormous wings covered the rest of its body. Each feather shone nacreous. Miniscule movements were enough to nearly blind me.

But it appeared entirely contained to the circle where, if my actions for the other representatives proved true, I must have summoned an Earl of Hell. Surely this was the same creature as the one that had hounded me? The hart-like demon turned by some illusion?

It had not answered my question.

"Tell me your name."

It cocked its head at me and smiled. The expression dazzled me. Not only were the teeth beautifully white, but the emotion it evoked was both sensual and somehow romantic. I felt like I had known the creature for eons, that it had my best interest at heart.

"My name?" it cooed. The voice that emerged was altogether different to the raspy, quick-spoken hart. This angel spoke slowly, with a resonant drawl. Not overly deep, but full-bodied, like an aged red wine. I opened my mouth to drink it in. "My name is Furfur."

"Furfur," I repeated. "You are an Earl of Hell?"

"A Great and Mighty Earl of Hell," it said. "And you are a little human whore."

I—hadn't expected that. I jolted in place as the incongruency of the angel's image and its words ran through me.

"My name is Alessandro."

A bright, happy laugh. "I could not care less what you call yourself. I can smell you from here. You reek of demonic sulphur, but your humanity's stench is stronger. Foul. What have you done to come here? How can you traverse this land without my brethren punishing you?" Its eyes flicked down my body, and its eyebrows raised. "Ah. I see someone has already attempted to punish you."

I flushed. I became overly aware of my body,

"Come here and let me help you."

"I am Asmodeus'," I clarified. "I am here on its order."

It raised its other brow at me until its look of disbelief was almost comical.

"I have heard no such thing."

"I believe that is part of the challenge, Earl Furfur."

It laughed again and opened its wings fractionally. I noticed a few feathers singed as they touched the invisible barrier of the circle's edge. Furfur tried in vain to keep the pain from its face, but that beautiful nose crinkled as it snapped its wing to its side.

I walked closer, confident it was contained.

"You can't get out of the circle?" I asked. Of course, it did not answer this. "Not until I tell you to?"

It glanced away, so I guessed I was right. Why this rule applied to Furfur and not the others, I could not be sure.

"Are you being punished?"

It snapped around. The angelic visage cracked; oozing blood leaked from its eyes, which had turned pitch black. The voice turned demonic, a thousand shouting cries at once as they screamed, "So many questions for a whore!" Its facade returned momentarily and that old, pleasant voice with it. "I should be asking *you* what gives you the right to gallivant about in mine territory."

I hesitated only momentarily but ended up telling it. What was the point in pretending to be anything other than what I was? I invoked Asmodeus, my Lord, at least four times, and each time Furfur sneered at me.

When I was done, it stared blankly at me before that placid face devolved into a grimace. It threw its head back and laughed so hard its body shook, wings bouncing by its side.

"Do you expect me to believe that, little human?" it snarled. Quickly, it pressed itself against the invisible barrier that kept it trapped within the circle. All those fine features scrunched against the delineation of the sigil's power, skin bunching up, nose upturned, mouth and teeth bared as it breathed heavily. The skin singed, and it hissed. "How could you have piqued the Lord's interest? Asmodeus is a King of Hell!"

Emboldened by my time with Furcas and, of course, by the safety granted by this sigil's power, I stepped close. I told Furfur, "Because I summoned it," and watched gleefully as its face fell. Curiously, Furfur tilted its head. The curled hair drooped to the side as it considered me in this new light.

"One of my brethren destroyed your body," it said quietly. "You must have convinced someone to fuck you. Lustful, abhorrent human—I'm surprised by your persuasion."

"Furcas did that to me," I said and watched as Furfur raised a brow. It did not hide its interest in that and grinned broadly.

"Furcas? That ridiculous primordial cunt." It spat the last word through its overly large smile. "It would not touch a human."

"Unless. . .?" I prompted.

Furfur's face fell. Inexplicably, in seconds, it drew its wings around itself. The white feathers shone as they slotted against one another, and soon I could see nothing of the angelic form beneath. Furfur was. . .hiding from me.

This lasted nearly half an hour. At first, I tried to speak to it, to encourage it to converse with me. But it was thinking, or sulking; I knew not the nature of demons and had found they weren't consistent creatures. For whatever reason, Furfur did not wish to look upon me whilst it ruminated.

I drew away from it and lay down on the hot rock, letting it think and deciding I would stay there as long as it took. Asmodeus had tasked this of me, and so long as the sigil held, Furfur would be trapped. In the meantime, I set about trying to feel what was happening in my lower body. I spread my legs and reached around to feel the smooth, sensitive insides that had spilled out. It twitched as I tensed, half curling back towards the anus but not slipping back inside.

I flushed because I knew then that I would need help, and when I looked up, Furfur was looking back.

Its face was the picture of innocence, all upturned brows and gently pursed lips. It tilted its head as its wings sank behind its back. Quickly, I stood up.

Furfur said, "I have been thinking."

"Yes, I gathered that."

A beat passed. It looked me up and down. "What happens to me if I touch you?"

I frowned. What? "Nothing. Except, I suppose, a bit of pleasure."

"And what happens to me if I don't?"

Without thinking I replied, "I'm much more concerned about what happens to *me*. Lord Asmodeus tasked this of me. I won't be allowed at its side without pleasuring a demon from every rank."

It looked—defeated. Suddenly, I was hit by the softness of its tone. It had sounded so sincere, then, like a youthful young man. Like Oliviero, worried about forgetting a passage he had meant to memorise. But this—Furfur's voice had a tinge of fear.

Then, stepping forward, I clarified with, "What are you afraid will happen?"

To my surprise, it answered immediately. "It is as you said before. I am being punished. Where my brethren's circles summons them alone, mine binds me to the summoner.

I realised what it was saying belatedly. "You are worried I will force you?"

And I was floored.

At once, all of my Biblical studies rose up against me. It felt as if I had been punched.

Do not ask me why it had not crossed my mind before. Everything I had done in Hell, whether I had resisted out of fear or not, I had wanted; I had consented to in my heart of hearts. But the teachings rose in me, phrases and passages that had caught the morality in my mind raised up again.

The covenant of marriage became a bulwark against immoral action; marriage itself was all the consent a man could ever need to touch his wife. Sex was a duty for so many of the Christians I knew. In the community I had preached to, it had happened many a time.

If he forced himself upon her, was it rape, when Proverbs 5:19 said he could have her "at all times"? When 1 Corinthians 7:4 said, "A wife does not have the right over her own body, but her husband does"?

*"Therefore as the church is subject unto Christ, so let the wives be to their own husbands **in every thing**."*

Ephesians 5:24 (KJV)

Sex was a martial debt that was owed; it was not about mutual pleasure, it was not about love, it was not about consent. I realised with a dawning horror what kind of God I had served for so long, where even the demons that had used me until breaking point had done so because I had sought them out willingly.

Tears were in my eyes when I looked up at Furfur. "I will not ask anything of you that you do not wish. But I will ask you to direct me to another Earl so that I might fulfil my duty to the Lord Asmodeus."

Furfur looked at me and tilted its head. "Why do you cry? Do you want me inside you that badly?"

It made me laugh just slightly. I put aside my sympathy and shook my head. "For what are you being punished?"

"I am reckless. Chaotic. Asmodeus has made it so I must tell the truth when summoned. Our Lord has prevented me from tricking humans so easily."

Then, this sigil made it vulnerable, and its attempts to hide from me behind its wings appeared as reactions to that awful feeling I knew all too well.

"Furfur, I will let you go if you tell me where to find another Earl."

"And what if I don't want you to find another Earl?"

"Why. . ." I did not know what question to ask. Why are you like this? Why are you chaotic, and deceiving, and why does it seem like you're frightened of me? I was stumped by this indecisive attitude, which did not align with my under-standing of demons at all.

Furfur saw through all of this. "Because I am bored, little human. Bored out of my mind. A millennium has passed with nothing interesting happening. You and your arrival here is the most exciting thing in an age. But I do not like humans; I cannot separate the reality of where I live now from where I used to live, the reality of who I am now from who I used to be. It does not matter that ages of men have risen and fallen or that I am so different now from the angel I once was. There is a part of me that craves the comfort of Heaven without God's tyranny, but He was always a tyrant, and Heaven was never as soft as I believed it to be. I did not wish to bow for humans. I still do not wish it."

"I am not asking you to bow for me," I said. "I will release you from this circle. I am asking you to put me in my place."

This sparked something in Furfur's eyes. The beautiful angelic face flushed, and light sparkled in its eyes. "I want to put you in your place."

My breath hitched. I flexed my fingers by my side,

fighting to keep my voice steady. "Then you'll help me?" It wavered anyway, with hope and desire.

Furfur did not answer. It was bound to tell the truth, so I gathered its silence was a kind of truth; uncertainty. I smiled somewhat at that, amused by the thought of sanctions on demons, though the smile faded quickly. Then I asked it to tell me more about itself. It did not react well to this at first; its wings flared up as if to shield its face and body from my scrutiny once more. But with a placating hand and a few words, I managed to ask it carefully, "Tell me about the hierarchy. Tell me how you came to be an Earl."

Furfur stood straighter as pride bolted through it. I saw momentarily the kind of angel it might have been, the sin of its self-interest that had led it to follow Lucifer Morningstar into a war.

"Earl is my title. We were the many angels who joined the rebellion against God after we saw higher and mightier angels launching the assault. They did not tremble in fear of the Almighty; they attacked without remorse. We were the ones who bolstered the ranks. Lucifer granted us this title to recognise that service."

I felt my walls falling. I expected. . .something different from Furfur, or from demons in general; it told me it was a liar and a deceiver, and I could feel my empathy encompassing it in an embrace. Some voice told me not to trust it, but I trusted Asmodeus more than myself; I trusted that my Lord would not allow me to suffer unduly.

"Put me in my place, Furfur," I murmured.

It flashed me a look, those large hazel eyes growing watery, expression soft and sweet beneath those long lashes. It wet its lips. "Is that a command?"

"A request," I clarified. "Only if you wish it."

We stared at one another, and eventually, the angelic creature shook out its hair. The shiver went through its whole body, each feather rustling and fluffing up, and it drew its wings away from its body.

It revealed to me genderless perfection. I saw the supple chest, which was without nipples, the body smooth and soft and without a navel. My eyes cast lower, glancing off its hairless stomach to its genitals, which very plainly did not exist in any way I could comprehend. Gone was the abnormally fluffy cock of the hart form Furfur had previously taken. There was a smooth, firm mound that curved beneath its stomach, similar to a doll's form. Its legs were rounded, thighs soft and large. Alabaster smooth, like youth untouched.

My attraction to it proved complicated almost immediately. I felt interest tug in my belly, but there was a strangeness to the feeling. Part of me desired to gender Furfur, to seek out masculinity in its form and use that as a crutch on which to anchor my desire. But this was not what Furfur was. Indeed, it was what any of the demons were—neither man, nor woman, nor human. They were creatures whose bodies were moulded to change into forms I could recognise. This choice I would not take from Furfur. I would not ask it to appear as something else for me.

"How can I pleasure you?" I whispered. So much of my understanding of pleasure related to genitals; I craved to milk demons until they writhed with joy. Other erogenous parts of the body I comprehended as added benefits, ways to increase the feeling in the main areas I was set to touch.

Furfur smiled a dazzling smile. Its teeth were perfectly aligned and beautifully straight, teeth like freshly anchored pearly headstones, all in a row.

"Carnal pleasure does not interest me," the Earl said. "But I am interested in. . ."

Its eyes dropped to me—to my cock. Once again, I was hit by the terror of having my pleasure accounted for. I flushed immediately. "I—that was *not* what Lord Asmodeus meant. I am to pleasure others, not—"

"And what if this gives me pleasure?" Furfur's teeth turned strange and sharp, fangs growing from red gums. It bared them to me, shoving its face against the barrier. "To reduce a human to a mewling, wanton mess with only my hands and my mouth? To take the form of an angel and sour that beauty with carnal depravity? What if it bolsters both my mood and my self-image to remember much of humanity is so easily tempted by matters of the flesh?" Furfur pressed close against the barrier until those fine features were pressed and stretched almost humorously. "What if your puny human mind cannot comprehend my desires? What if something as simple as orgasm does nothing for me after eons? You can't possibly understand; you are still an infant in your discovery. So do not presume to tell me what it is I desire!"

Its voice raised to a howling shriek, and I shied away from the noise. My heart ached in my chest from the speed of this change, and another part *enjoyed* it. The blasphemer in me saw the angelic form and shivered with equal parts revulsion and thrill. But I enjoyed, too, the layered truth. Beneath this beauty was a demon who, like me, had turned its back on God. Who enjoyed playing with forms, who in part still clung to its angelic identity—who understood implicitly that the most depraved thing I could imagine would always involve religion.

"I—apologise," I said, and Furfur's wrath withered away in moments. Beauty returned; Furfur stepped back into its graceful form.

"Then?" it whispered. "Will you let me touch you? Let me drop your anxious, fleeting mind back into your body?"

"Yes," I said. "Step out of the circle."

And so it did.

As if there had never been a barrier, Furfur daintily

stepped over the circle's grooves. Each step had a grace to it, a deliberate and measured approach. It looked up at me, its head lowered so half of its face was covered by its long curls. Those beautiful wings wrapped around its body, and only when it was close to me did it stretch them out wide, wide, *wide* until a great shadow fell upon us. Furfur reached out to me with strange gentleness, a hand on my waist as it pulled me close.

Very softly, it kissed me.

CHAPTER ELEVEN

I went rigid. My heart raced, and my hands grew clammy with sweat. Emotions clashed in my mind—was I enjoying this? Was I afraid? Was this anxiety and anticipation, or was the way my stomach tilted because I found this unpleasant?

I realised I wasn't sure. For me, pleasure had always been rough, sometimes violent; I understood the primal urge better than I understood intimacy. Furfur kissed me slowly, lips urging mine apart to drag its wet tongue against mine. Slowly, slowly, like the first hint of snowfall, a flake drifting to the ground as it's carried by the wind—this was what kissing Furfur felt like. I forgot it was a demon. I felt the brush of feathers against my neck as its wing wrapped around the two of us. It smelt like sea brine and vanilla. The hand around my waist pulled me ever closer, and I—hesitant, shaking—dared to raise my hand to its cheek.

I had never been kissed like this. I had never been kissed without the urge behind it; I had never been kissed for the sake of being kissed.

"You are frightened," it whispered as it pulled away from

me, and though its voice curled sweetly with concern, I could see the glimmer of joy in its eyes. It enjoyed me like this— enjoyed that I was vaguely uncomfortable.

"Yes. I. . ."

"You do not have to say it," it whispered, and it turned my head to the side to lick at my neck and my jaw.

It took minutes with me. Took its time. Whenever I reached up to press its head closer to me, whenever I bucked back, urging it to touch other parts of my body, it laughed sweetly and slowed its touches. Eventually, it began to lightly drag its fingers up and down my body. Once or twice, it thumbed over my nipple, but this was the most definitive touch I got for what seemed like an hour. It ran its fingers over my belly, skimmed over my hips and caressed close to my twitching cock, fingertips gentle as they teased. Indeed, Furfur *was* teasing; I could hear on occasion a gentle laugh and see a pleased smile curling at its lips in my periphery. I tried to hold myself still against this tamed assault, but by Asmodeus, I craved more.

I whined. I bucked and twisted and twitched about; I leaned into this pathetic display to increase my chances of Furfur accidentally touching somewhere that desperately needed the friction.

"Stop that," Furfur growled into my ear, sweet voice peeling back to reveal something more eager, more feral than it was letting on. A hand coiled up around my neck, and it pressed against the sides of my throat. "Lie down."

I went to my knees first, practically thrashing out of Furfur's grip in the hopes of speeding this along. It commanded me to turn, and I did, laying back on the warm stone and bringing my knees up.

Furfur went onto its knees, too, and those beautiful wings encompassed the pair of us like a shroud as they encircled us, a wing coming down on either side of my head. It leaned forward, hands planted beside my face, and brought itself down to kiss me.

The kiss and this position were almost adolescent; I wondered if this was what it would have been like if I had fumbled about with a boy in my youth.

"You are to do nothing but enjoy yourself," Furfur purred to me. "Enjoy yourself to the point of delirium. But do not fake it, little human. I will know if you are lying to me."

My stomach sank. Distantly, I became aware that I had intended just that; to draw on memories and throw myself about in pleasure because the lie behind those actions made them safer to me than my true reactions. It brought a hand to cup my cheek and urged me to nod. I did, resting only slightly against the support its palm offered.

Then, it began to kiss me again. My eyes fluttered closed. It was so much easier that way, easier to relax, easier to pretend I was alone. The act of being seen unnerved me. When I was being *had*, when I was being *used*, it did not matter how I writhed or screamed. Those things did not embarrass me because I was there for another's pleasure. But when the focus fell upon me, I grew afraid that all my failings and my ugliness would be on display. I grew frightened that the act of pleasuring me would grow boring or that whomever or whatever was touching me would realise spending time elsewhere would suit them better. I grew afraid that if I let my walls down enough to feel my body and the pleasure in it, I would grow to resent myself. Firstly, for what I had become and the vulgarity of it—for shame still lingered in my blood, no matter how many demons tried to fuck it out of me. Or perhaps it would be revealed that my enjoyment mattered to no one, that my use was in being a hole and nothing more. But more importantly, perhaps, I would grow to resent how frightened I had been—I was almost more scared about being *wrong*. In enjoying the act of my pleasure, in focusing on my body, in taking the time to touch it and enjoy it for *only* me, I would realise again how long I had waited. I would learn something uncomfortable about myself during the act, and I would realise I had more worth than the flesh I offered others to fuck.

What then? What if, somewhere in this act, I realised I had made a mistake coming here?

Furfur must have felt the speed of my pulse against its lips; I could practically feel the vein throbbing with speed.

"Shhh," Furfur cooed to me. "Think of nothing but my lips on you. Feel nothing except the pleasure of it. Stay grounded in this moment, little lamb. Do not let your mind grow foggy with your fear."

It—was a hard ask, but I tried. I focused on the way Furfur's fingers touched me, on the smell of its wings and the way those feathers sometimes grazed across my outflung arms. The creature wet its mouth and licked gently down my body, each touch firm and deliberate but without fervour behind it. It took a nipple into its mouth, sucking gently, its tongue rolling over it. The other nipple was placed between forefinger and thumb to squeeze gently, twist this way and that and tugging occasionally, but never so hard I cried out in pain. Just enough pressure to send jolts of pleasure tingling down into my core. My cock grew steadily thicker, and I tried to reach down and *squeeze* there—except Furfur stopped me, not harshly. It shushed me again and stroked its fingers over my stomach. I let my head fall back, and I closed my eyes as it teased and touched me.

It dropped lower over minutes, tonguing me, stroking me. My breathing went erratic as I shivered and jolted beneath it. Then it moved lower until its mouth was hovering over my cock.

I craned to look down at it. What a thing of beauty. It stared at me through heavy-lidded eyes, its curls tickling my lower stomach and inner thighs. The sight of that alone made my cock throb. It jumped towards Furfur's mouth, which parted slightly. Its lips were stained a pinkish red, and a flush had crept onto its cheeks. I wanted to call out to God, suddenly—for this face was so beautiful, so angelic, I almost forgot where I was and who I had pledged myself to. Very carefully, the angelic-looking demon wrapped a hand around my cock, pulled down the foreskin, and brought its lips over the glands.

I moaned roughly. Furfur only laughed lightly, pulling back to lick sensually at the slit where precum had gathered and begun to ooze free. At my side, I balled my fists, gripping nothing but my own flesh. Anticipation tugged like a string in my belly, and I grunted as I watched Furfur wet its mouth again, pooling saliva on its tongue. It looked up at me and swallowed my cock whole.

"*Oh, fu. . .*" I bit off the word, hand shaking as I reached down to pull the demon's head closer. At a slow and gentle pace, Furfur dragged its mouth up and down my length, tongue stroking every which way as it went. Furfur moaned, too, each time I did, and its left hand reached up to pat my belly. A touch of. . .affection? Intimacy?

Tears sprang up, not of pain but of fear. I felt suddenly exposed in a way I hated, like the skin of my stomach was being slowly pulled back, and all my insides were being picked up, inspected, and set steaming onto the ground. I could have been sick, then. I almost wanted to roll over and force myself to vomit, though I had eaten nothing but the flower and fluids of demons for however long I'd been there. Anything to expel this feeling in me. Anything to disrupt the vulnerability and the shame and the fear of letting myself relax into pleasure.

"Do not cry," Furfur whispered to me, and it brought its wings even closer to frame my face.

I heard my voice. The wings around my head became like a cave, a chamber within which my voice echoed back to me.

"Enjoy yourself, Alessandro. Enjoy yourself."

I did not understand what was happening, but I heard muffled song behind the blockade of wings, a beautiful choral sound. A thousand angels in unison holding a single holy note; my vision went briefly white, and my body relaxed.

Furfur murmured, *"Weeping may tarry for the night, but joy comes with the morning."*

It was Pslam 30:5. I think it was trying to tell me my discomfort was a fleeting thing, but the passage meant something different. I opened my mouth to argue, managing, "That's not—" before it swallowed my cock whole again.

I threw my head back. It began to suck and lick in earnest. Saliva fell from its mouth in wet strings, and soon, even my balls were slick. Gently, it moved its forefinger and thumb up and down the base, the rest of its mouth sucking dutifully. I lost time like that, panting and moaning, and every time the pleasure built, it would slow down, start licking gently and out of any discernible rhythm until I grew frustrated and cried out, trying to force its head back onto my length.

Furfur laughed again. The tone bordered on triumphant; it was glad it was making me like this. Then, unprompted, it lowered its mouth—to my prolapsed hole.

I jolted, having completely forgotten about the state of my body.

"I—"

"Hush," Furfur said before it began to suck and lick, tonguing up into the hole. I shivered, confused by the pleasure that overrode the discomfort. I clenched instinctively and felt myself try to tighten. Then, Furfur put its hand against the flesh and *pushed.*

"Ah!" I gasped, bucking up. It pushed and pushed until I was sure its whole fist was inside me.

"It's back in," Furfur whispered, though it did not take its hand out. It began to move gently, scraping my insides but barely deep. With only this small amount of friction, I was surprised by how good it felt, and when Furfur lowered its mouth again to suck at me, my consciousness and mind went black with pleasure.

The pressure built almost immediately. The feeling of being full, hole clenching over the angel's knuckles, was nearly enough to make me cum. But then I looked down and watched my cock disappearing into that angelic mouth, watched those long eyelashes flutter as Furfur moaned, watched those reddish lips pucker and suck, and I thought: *yes*. Yes. This pleasure, this desire, was new. I wanted to fuck deeper into Furfur's throat. I wanted to hear the angel gag and groan; I wanted to know what an angel looked like with human seed dripping over its face. And so I bucked up. I grabbed the back of Furfur's head firmly and shoved it down. The angelic body convulsed, wings shuddering, and I heard it gag and splutter. I expected resistance, but the angel—the demon—just *took it*.

"Oh, you slut," I whispered, feeling as every demon must have felt fucking me. Its eyes rolled back into its head, alabaster cheeks flushed pink and saliva drooling from its mouth. It moaned and tried to move its head again, to choke itself on my cock.

"No," I grunted and held its head in place. "Stay there. Let me use you."

And Furfur did. Obediently, it held its head in place, letting me wrap both hands around its skull to fuck desperately into that warm, wet hole. Sloppy sounds escaped from its mouth, in amongst its groans and my heavy, eager breathing. It brought its wings around me, tighter like an embrace, and I heard in clear detail all my airy moans and sweet sounds. The chorus of angels still sang; theirs a united chorus. I felt urged on in an almost holy way, like embracing this side of me that so obviously desired pleasure was endorsed by the Heavens.

Yes, I thought I heard Asmodeus itself whisper. *Yes, look at you, my little priest. Look how desperate you are. Look how pleased this makes you. You take your pleasure from others the same way you ask it to be taken from you. Every part of you desires filth. Go and make whores of my demons as they will make a whore of you. Let us all revel in pleasure together.*

This endorsement made me snap my hips even faster until I was forcing myself down Furfur's throat, and its grip on my stomach became desperate. It gagged and convulsed, and I was certain it would vomit, certain I was suffocating it—and it did not matter. All I cared about at that moment was cumming.

"*Yes, yes, yes,*" I began to whisper. The pleasure built and built, and glory fell upon me, and just at the crux, I pulled out to the sound of Furfur gasping for air, and its beautiful lips were wet with stringy saliva, eyes trembling heavenward, and the angel looked so pathetic and wanton that I came violently over its face.

I cried out, and as I did, Furfur echoed me, and in that moment of unity, lightning and thunder crashed around us, the world going bright like Hell itself shivered in orgasmic pleasure, the earth experiencing the delight of my flesh.

I gasped and panted for what felt like an eternity before I brought myself to look upon Furfur. It watched me and carefully began to drag its forefinger across its face, lapping up my cum. One eye had been streaked with it, and its eyelashes appeared sticky and heavy when it tried to open its eye. I moaned again at that sight. I had done that to this angel. To this demon.

Once it had cleaned itself, Furfur dragged itself over me and kissed me. Its breath smelled of cock and saliva and sex, and I kissed it hungrily, exhausted and pleasured and about as happy I had ever been.

And I realised belatedly what Furfur had allowed of me—that how it had made me wanton and begging was to transform my pleasure. It had allowed me the act of subjugating *it*, rather than putting me in my place, as I had offered it.

It was almost—a kindness.

Except in truth, what Furfur had done was confirm my place here. Gone was the anxiety and the fear of not belonging. Furfur seemed to recognise this itself, for it smiled wide, and its form shivered back to that demonic hart.

I did not care. I let the creature rest upon my chest and stroked its furred head. And in that comfortable, pleasured silence, Furfur opened its mouth and began to laugh.

I was so used to the strangeness of demons that I did not react. I lay there and kept stroking it, even when it began to say, "Human whore. You cannot turn away from your nature."

"No," I agreed. "I cannot."

Furfur sat up then and looked down upon me, its eyes deep reflective pools of black, like polished onyx. "Lord Asmodeus rarely does this, though you are not the first human it has tested. Only. . ."

I sat up after it. "Only?"

Furfur twisted its head to the side and nuzzled against my cheek. Its fleshy, moulting antlers rested against my head. "Only you are different, little priest. You are interesting. And your desire is so palpable it cannot be ignored. It was your destiny to come here. Your destiny to betray God and to give your body to us."

I said nothing to this, and Furfur did not press me. I looked down at its changed form and saw that fluffy cock waiting. I raised my hand. Furfur slapped me away.

"This form is deceiving," Furfur whispered. "But I still lack that desire."

I nodded, questioning silently why I had reached out.

Because you wish to return the favour. Because you can't take for the sake of taking, and you don't know how to act without offering your body in return.

"Tsk, tsk," Furfur said. "You haven't learnt. But perhaps that's what I can take from this: your discomfort. I want you to itch knowing you could not, under any circumstance, satisfy my body."

My lip curled in distaste at that, though looking back now, Furfur was still being kind. Empathy, I felt, was something Furfur possessed, even if it had been twisted drastically over eons in this realm.

"I want to serve Asmodeus for the rest of my days," I whispered, and then I fell silent. Why was I saying this? What did I want? Awkwardly, I cleared my throat. "I. . .do you think that I will. . ."

The hart looked at me. "You will be well used, little lamb," Furfur said. "Well used. The Lord will take your flesh whenever it pleases, and you will enjoy that for the rest of time."

A comfort again, an odd one. Its fiery tail made its furred head glow orange. Then it stood and spread its leathery wings.

"The Lord Asmodeus is making you known to us in this way," Furfur announced. "This is a great blessing, even if you do not understand it yet."

I sat up straighter and opened my mouth, but Furfur launched from the ground and flew away, and the waves below us ceased their noise, and the clouds dispersed, and I was left on that rocky platform alone to ponder.

EPILOGUE

Like this, I had passed through three of the devilish realms and had a further three to go before I would come before Asmodeus.

Thinking on this, I began to pray to the Lord:

I am a servant to you, O Lord. I will do your bidding. And no matter to what I must subject myself, no matter the embarrassment I must endure, no matter anything in this realm, I will fulfill the promise.

I will become whatever you need me to be.

For nearly half an hour, I prayed like this, overwhelmed with a spiritual devotion that had nowhere to go except to be funnelled in prayer to my Lord's ears.

It took that long for Asmodeus to answer me, a beautiful sound to rally me forward.

"Alessandro, my little priest, my whore, my beautiful blasphemer. Come to me. Come to me. Devote yourself eternally. Let us show God together why pleasure and sin and temptation is the way to live. Let us revolt against His tyranny for eternity. Come and be my pet, my toy, my devoted slut."

My heart grew to bursting with devotion.

"Yes," I answered aloud. *Yes, yes, yes.*

With purpose, and devotion, and love blooming in my chest, I stood up.

A further three demons to find and to pleasure, and then I would be Asmodeus'. Everything I had wanted for thirty-five years would be mine.

A deity to worship, a body used and appreciated and pleasured, a purpose I could fulfill.

Life was worth it. Every struggle had led to this.

It was Romans 12:12 that came to mind, then, a passage from God's word that felt appropriate here, that I could twist to suit my new life.

"Rejoice in hope, be patient in tribulation, be constant in prayer."

To all things, lust. To all things, pleasure.

To all things, Asmodeus.

END

ABOUT THE AUTHOR

Lucien Burr has a background in Classics and is an author of dark fiction. His previous works include THE TERAS TRIALS and the PRINCE OF LUST series.

instagram.com/lucienburr